"We need to set some ground rules first."

"About what?"

"About you and me," she said, crossing her arms over her ribs and glowering at him. "About boundaries."

He inclined his head. "Go on."

"I won't sleep with you again," she said, her eyes flashing with fierce heat. "And you're not welcome in my home."

He held her gaze for a silent beat, and then dipped his attention to her mouth and breasts for the faintest flicker of time before returning, "Don't fret. I have no plans to join you in your bed."

Color seeped into her cheeks. "Good."

Because soon you'll be begging to join me in mine.

And this time she wouldn't leave until he told her to go.

All about the author...
Natasha Tate

NATASHA TATE'S romantic side has its roots in childhood. Ask anyone and you'll hear she spent too many of her formative years believing she was Cinderella. This despite the fact that she had two loving parents and no evil stepmother in sight. Her earliest drawings were of princess attire, replete with bows, ribbons and multiple flounces. She warbled about her future prince during chores, and began each night by assuming the most earnest Sleeping Beauty pose.

Alas, school did not tolerate such fanciful notions, and she quickly learned to rely on romance novels to satisfy her cravings for happy endings. As an army brat and perennial new kid, she consumed a book a day, hiding them within her textbooks while training half an ear on her teachers' lectures. This habit persisted into college, despite her more traditional academic pursuits, equipping her with the skills needed to tame her own alpha-male hero.

Now that she's married and the mother of three strapping sons, Natasha's experiencing her own happily ever after. As an author for Harlequin Books, she lives her dream of crafting fairy-tale romances set in modern-day, larger-than-life settings. Visit her at www.NatashaTate. com, or email her at Natasha@NatashaTate.com.

Books by Natasha Tate

Harlequin Presents®

Other titles by this author available in eBook

Natasha Tate

ONCE TOUCHED,
NEVER FORGOTTEN

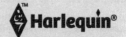

TORONTO NEW YORK LONDON
AMSTERDAM PARIS SYDNEY HAMBURG
STOCKHOLM ATHENS TOKYO MILAN MADRID
PRAGUE WARSAW BUDAPEST AUCKLAND

Recycling programs
for this product may
not exist in your area.

ISBN-13: 978-0-373-13034-4

ONCE TOUCHED, NEVER FORGOTTEN

First North American Publication 2011

ONCE TOUCHED,
NEVER FORGOTTEN

To my dear husband and boys,
who've supported me every step of the way.

CHAPTER ONE

No.

Shocked denial cinched Colette's stomach into a tight knot and she couldn't seem to draw a proper breath. As she stared at the telltale blue line, the second in as many hours, Colette's trembling hands nearly dropped the evidence she wanted so desperately to deny.

How had this happened?

It doesn't matter. It's happened.

She couldn't avoid the truth any longer. One test might lie. But two? Never. Shaking, and feeling slightly ill, she placed the plastic testing wand on her flat's scarred bathroom counter and then braced her quivering arms against the sink.

She was pregnant.

With Stephen Whitfield's child.

Colette closed her eyes, leaned her forehead against the cool mirror, and tried to think through her options.

As if she had any.

She knew Stephen. She knew his plans for the future, and they didn't include her. They never had. How many times had he told her of his decision to never marry or have children? He liked his solitary life, loved his freedom. It allowed him to focus on business without messy, emotional distractions.

Through a tacit, unspoken agreement, neither of them had pressed for more. Neither had asked questions the other didn't wish to answer. The past remained in the past; they lived for the moment. It was safer that way. For today, for the duration of their affair, he'd accepted her, pleasured her, and made her feel wanted. She'd told herself it was enough.

And it had been enough.

Until she'd fallen in love.

Closing her eyes, she inhaled sharply. She couldn't change the rules on him. She wouldn't. They'd been too careful to avoid talk of each other's pasts, too careful to make no demands the other wouldn't wish to fill. Though she suspected he carried scars no mere female could heal, she certainly was in no position to try. She wouldn't be naïve enough to offer.

But you're going to have his child.

It didn't matter.

No way would she be one of those women who trapped a man into marriage by getting herself pregnant. No way would she repeat her mother's mistakes and put her child in the middle of a loveless marriage. And she knew Stephen well enough to know that he'd demand just that. He'd forfeit his future for his child, and then hate them both because of it.

Curving a hand over her abdomen, she felt a rush of protectiveness bring the sting of tears to her eyes. It didn't matter that her baby's father had no desire for children. It didn't matter that their fling was supposed to be a temporary indulgence with no strings. No expectations. No future.

She'd make her child feel loved regardless of the circumstances of her conception. No baby of hers would ever feel like a pawn in a marriage built on coercion, obligation and resentment.

She had to break things off with Stephen. Today.

And she had to make it believable.

Forty minutes later, she stepped from Stephen's private elevator and walked into his absent secretary's front reception area. For once, Colette was grateful not to have to talk to the friendly but nosy older woman. She didn't think she'd be able to feign cheerfulness just now.

The Whitfield Grand's thick carpet muffled her footsteps as she continued toward Stephen's office, making Colette's thudding pulse sound far too loud by comparison. Feeling like she'd swallowed ten pounds of lead, and with her mouth as dry as flour, she approached his open doors along the left wall of the reception area.

She heard Stephen's voice, raised in a heated argument with two other men whose voices she didn't recognize, and stalled just outside his door.

"Grandfather," Stephen said, the subtle evidence of his temper edging his delivery. "You're making assumptions that have no basis in fact."

"Don't take that tone with me," barked the Whitfield patriarch. "And don't talk to me about *facts*. My sources are impeccable."

"Your sources are wrong."

"She may as well have you fitted with a nose ring, the way you let her lead you around."

Colette's pulse picked up speed. Were they discussing *her*?

"You're in so deep," seconded a third male, his tone nasally and weak, "you don't even notice other women."

"I'm not in *deep*, Liam," Stephen ground out. "But even if I were, whomever I choose to notice is no concern of yours."

"The hell it isn't!" snapped his grandfather. "Would you get your head out of your pants and *think* for a minute? Whether you deserve it or not, you're a Whitfield, and everything you do reflects on us. I won't have you making a mess of things like your idiot father did."

"Keep my father out of this," Stephen warned in a low, dangerous tone.

"You need to cut the chit off before you get in over your head. Before you make a mistake you can't fix."

"I'm not cutting her off just because you think it's time," she heard Stephen say. "*I* decide when we're over, not you."

"As long as you *do* decide, I don't give a rat's ass when it happens. Sleep with her for another twenty years for all I care, just don't make the mistake of thinking she's wife material," said his grandfather in a flat, authoritative voice. "If you learned nothing from your father, learn that."

"She doesn't have what it takes to make a Whitfield wife," intoned Liam. "She never will."

"Who said she even wants to be a Whitfield?" Stephen shot back, sounding more irritated than she'd ever heard him.

"She'd be a fool not to," warned Liam. "Penniless nobodies never understand they're incapable of belonging in our world. You, more than anyone, must realize that."

"You're using protection, aren't you?" his grandfather continued, and Colette's stomach bottomed out.

We used protection every time.

"Get out of my office." When Stephen's anger turned to cold, controlled menace, his relatives would be smart to heed the warning.

"Don't tell me you trust her?" sputtered his grandfather, oblivious to the danger.

Stephen's silence lanced Colette's chest.

"He trusts her!" he exclaimed in audible disbelief. "Damn it, you're smarter than this! What if she gets pregnant?"

"She wouldn't." He ground the words through clenched teeth. "She knows I'd never bring another Whitfield into this world."

"Like that would stop her."

"It would," Stephen snapped. "She respects my boundaries, just like I respect hers."

He's right. She willed them to hear, remembering the walls she'd tried to erect between them. The barriers to intimacy she'd never wanted crossed. But then Stephen had stared at her with his scorching, sultry blue eyes and agreed to every demand she made, convincing her that she was the one in control even as he burned through her heart's icy layers.

Whitfield dismissed his grandson's claim with a patronizing grunt. "*All* women want commitment. How do you not know that?"

"Colette's different."

She'd thought she was, too. But she'd been wrong. She'd ended up loving him despite her vows not to, and now the pain of leaving him would be permanently lodged in her heart.

"She's smart enough to make you believe it," said Liam. "I'll give you that."

"And she's got legs that go for miles," added his grandfather. "So I can understand a bit of temporary blindness. But enough's enough. You're risking too much with that trash."

"You're done here," Stephen bit out. The telltale squeak of Stephen's chair as he pushed back from his desk was immediately followed by the protest of leather and wood as the two other men stood. "I suggest you leave. Now."

"This isn't over," Liam said, his voice moving closer to Colette.

Desperate not to be seen, Colette ducked behind the open door, squeezing silently between wood and wall while the Whitfields passed by. Her pulse thrashed noisily against her ears and she held her breath until the two men boarded the elevator and then descended out of sight.

Her breath escaped in a silent, unsteady thread and she closed her eyes, trying to regain her bearings. She stood without moving for several anguished minutes, or maybe it was hours, until her cell phone chimed against her thigh. Reaching to silence its betraying ring, her numb fingers fumbled and missed. It chimed again, the distinctive ringtone she'd set for Stephen making her stomach twist with dread.

"Colette?" Stephen called from his office, his chair squeaking again as he stood. "Are you out there?"

She lurched from behind the door, scuttling back toward

the elevator so she could approach his office as if she'd just arrived. Trepidation tightened her throat, but she forced a calm tone regardless. "Hey," she said when he appeared at his door, his dark head nearly brushing the top casing and his broad shoulders blocking the light from his windows.

He slid his phone into his pocket and strode toward her. "We must be on the same wavelength."

Before she had a chance to avoid him, he'd closed the space between them and reached for her. Both hands, wide and firm, threaded through her hair and tilted her mouth toward his, lifting her up to her toes. His lips caught hers and the lush warmth elicited the same shock of response it always did. Every part of her body reacted. Heated.

His scent and taste conspired to make her lose her focus, and for a moment she allowed herself to savor the delicious probing of his kiss, the commanding sweep of his palms as he stroked her back from shoulder to hip. She swayed unsteadily when he withdrew, his soft exhalation warming her half-open mouth.

"I missed you this morning," he said against her lips as he bumped her pelvis with his. "I missed waking up next to you."

She heard the smile behind his words and closed her eyes, mustering her strength. "I had to be at work early," she said. "I'm just heading back for the afternoon shift now."

He must have heard something in her voice, because the same concerned note that had lulled her into complacency suddenly colored his tone. Leaning back, he peered into her face. "So why are you here?" His blue eyes glittered with fresh fury while his jaw knotted. "Did my grandfather or cousin say something to you?"

Blinking against a sudden blur of tears, she sucked in a steadying breath. *Don't fall apart now. You can do that later.* "No. I just…I needed to talk to you," she managed, swallowing hard.

His hands drifted from her waist up to her arms, a hint of wariness clouding his expression. "About what?"

"I…" She inhaled his lovely scent, gulping air to no avail. She couldn't seem to stop her body from shaking. "I need to sit down."

Wordless, he ushered her into his large masculine office and over to the brown leather chair angled before his desk. He pressed her into it, his palms bracketing her upper arms. He squatted before her, his expression incrementally more concerned as his thumbs caressed the skin beneath her white T-shirt sleeves. "What is it?"

After a few moments of torturous silence, while she struggled to find the right words, he inhaled sharply and dropped his hands to the leather armrests.

"You want to break it off, don't you?" he said, his expression an inscrutable shield of blankness.

She dipped her head in a single nod and dropped her gaze to her tightly knit hands. "It's time."

He stared at her in silence for several long beats before speaking, his voice cool and remote where before it had been warm. "Care to tell me why?"

"We promised no questions." She hauled in a breath and forced herself to meet his blue eyes. "And we both knew this—"

"You're right," he interrupted, surging to his feet and walking toward the floor-to-ceiling windows that overlooked the Thames. "You don't owe me any explanations," he said in a clipped voice as he stared out over the sun-drenched water.

She stared at his wide shoulders, the crisp lines of his charcoal suit, and the sleek, muscled transition from buttock to leg. "This is what we agreed to," she started again. "Remember? We said—"

"I said you were right." He shoved his hands deep in his pockets and turned back to face her, the sunlight glinting blue against his black hair. "If you want to end things, I won't stand in your way."

His easy capitulation, expected as it was, still hurt more than she'd have thought possible. "Thank you."

"We never claimed this was supposed to last," he said in a harsh voice, while the muscles in his jaw twitched. His silk sleeves bunched up around his wrists and she could see the knots of his fists within his pockets. "I won't pressure you for more."

She tamped down a flutter of irrational hope. An irrational, crazy hope that he'd beg her to stay. To marry him. To bear his children no matter what the powerful Whitfield family thought about her suitability. "Do you want more?" she whispered.

"Is that what you think?" he asked, withdrawing his hands from his pockets and striding toward her with ominous swiftness. He leaned to grip her upper arms, his gaze trapping hers. "Do you think I want more?"

She forced herself to maintain eye contact, to keep her impossible dreams buried too deep to see. "Do you?"

"Of course I don't!" he said, releasing her as if he'd been stung.

She inhaled sharply, pressing her shoulderblades against the back of the chair while her hope died a swift, brutal death. She'd been right not to tell him. Right to break things off. It was better this way, to be the one who did the rejecting first. Even so, shards of pain dug deep and shallow breaths serrated the back of her throat.

"I don't want a messy nightmare of a relationship any more than you do. You know that."

"That's what I thought," she said, while a wail of pain knotted silently within her chest.

His brow furrowed as he drew to a stop at the far side of the desk and turned back to her, his expression a queer blend of apology and grim resolve. "Though I can see how you might have believed otherwise."

She looked at him without blinking, her mind racing with all the things that still remained unsaid.

"I've hardly been acting the part of cavalier, detached lover lately."

"No." She pushed the word through her tight throat, praying that she sounded normal. Aloof and indifferent and strong, despite the fact that her scarred heart had been wounded anew. "You haven't. But I haven't been, either. So I guess we're both to blame."

He stared at her, his blue eyes unreadable and the muscles in his jaw and neck taut. "This hasn't been a typical fling for either one of us."

It's been my only fling. A fling that's left me pregnant. "No." She'd thought with Stephen, a notorious playboy who used women for pleasure and then discarded them without a backward glance, she could keep her heart safe. She'd thought that with her eyes open and her boundaries firmly in place she could indulge in a passionate affair without getting hurt.

She'd been wrong.

"I've barely given you a minute to yourself these past few months," he finally said.

"No."

"And it's hard to find the space we need to think when we're on top of each other all the time."

When she remained quiet, her heart thrashing like a wounded bird beneath her ribs, he rounded the desk and squatted before her yet again.

"What I'd prefer," he said quietly, as his intent gaze searched hers, "before we rush into anything drastic, is a little time apart to reassess. We don't have to end things right now. This minute. We can take some breathing room and decide how to move forward once we get our bearings."

"Move forward?" she whispered, her pulse rioting hard within her chest. Her throat. Her hands.

"Damn it. I know that's the wrong way to phrase it," he said, straightening again and running a hand through his hair. "But I'm not finished with you yet."

"Not *finished* with me?" she repeated in a thin voice.

"That's not what I meant. What I…" His voice trailed off with a muttered curse. "Hell, I don't know. I just know I like how we are together. Can't we just keep things the way they are?"

How could they keep things the way they were when he had no desire for more? When she was going to give birth to his child, *their* child, in a few frightfully short months?

"It's good, what we have. Isn't it?" He bent to collect her unresisting hands. "Just because we're never getting married or angling for that whole happy family illusion doesn't mean we can't enjoy the benefits of each other's company. There has to be a way that we can keep things the way they are without getting all tense and emotional about it." His eyes searched hers. "Right?"

"I…"

"I have to go to Paris for a couple of weeks, and it sounds like the timing couldn't be better." He pulled her up from the chair and hauled her close for another swift, bruising kiss, his hands gripping her upper arms with tensile strength. Withdrawing enough to study her expression, he stared deeply into her eyes. "We'll find something that works for both of us when I get back. I promise. Just don't make any big decisions until I return."

There were no big decisions to make, because they had already been made for her. She'd never agree to keep what they had, not if he had no desire for more. She had a child to think about now. A child who deserved more than a father who viewed happy families as illusions and thought love made things too *tense* and *emotional*.

No matter how much it hurt, she had to be realistic. Sex was not love, and she wasn't foolish enough to confuse the two. Rejection and hatred were hard enough for an adult to manage; it was unbearable torture for a small child who wanted nothing more than to be loved.

So she remained silent, her insides trembling with the realization that she'd never risk putting her sweet little baby through the pain she'd been subjected to. She'd die first. And if it that meant being alone forever, she'd do it. As a mother with a child to protect, she couldn't allow herself to entertain thoughts of romance or fairytale endings. Men who didn't want to be fathers had no place in her or her child's precious life.

CHAPTER TWO

Five years later

"I HAVE mixed feelings about this, Whitfield," said the soon-to-be former owner of the Renaissance Hotel, as he signed his name on the last of the purchasing paperwork. He slid the deed across the desk separating them and sighed. "This place has been my life for a long, long time."

"Yes," Stephen said as he added his own signature to the deed. "But it's a good decision. You've earned a decent retirement."

"Then why do I feel like I'm abandoning my family?"

"Trust me," Stephen assured the old man. "I will take care of your people."

Unlike the other hoteliers with whom he'd negotiated, Bill Masters' primary concern when it came to selling his aging property had been his employees. He didn't care about Stephen's money, the new business model he'd brought to the table, or any of the changes he intended to make. Masters only wanted his tribe of employees to be protected. It was an admirable sentiment, but it had made the transaction unnecessarily complicated.

"That's the only reason I sold to you," Masters reminded Stephen. "Because you agreed to keep them all on."

"Yes, I know." Stephen bit back an exasperated sigh.

Were it not for the Renaissance's prime New York location, overlooking Central Park, and its potential for profitability, Stephen would have abandoned the deal weeks ago. "As long as the employees perform their jobs efficiently, they have no reason to be concerned."

"But you'll be patient with them as they adjust to the new ownership?" Masters insisted.

"Of course," he said. It had never been his style to eviscerate a failing hotel and its staff just because he'd decided to finance its recovery. And, after purchasing and renovating eight different hotels in the last five years, he'd have thought his reputation would be enough to reassure the old man. Apparently, he'd been wrong. "It costs money to interview, hire and train new employees. Why would I incur the expense if it's not necessary?"

"It can't be just about the money," Masters reminded him, before lifting a large stack of manila folders to the desktop. "It has to be about the people. Their lives and their families and their dreams for the future. You'll be part of that now, and you'll need to look out for them."

"Yes," he repeated. "I'm aware of that." He'd navigated the rocky shores of staff relationships for too many years to *not* be aware of the impact his decisions had on the minutiae of their lives. He certainly didn't need some old man lecturing him on how to manage his employees successfully.

"These are the staff's updated personnel files," Masters said. "I thought we might go through so you can match a few faces with their names when you meet them."

As if he needed the directive. "Have you informed them about the transfer of ownership yet?"

The white-haired man cleared his throat and avoided Stephen's eyes, a dull red flush rising to color his neck. "I didn't think it wise to rush things."

Stephen arched a single brow. It wasn't like he was adopting the Renaissance employees, whether Masters wanted it to be that way or not. He was simply taking over as their boss. It was business. "It would have been better to disclose things earlier," he said grimly, barely concealing his annoyance. "They'd have had time to adjust to the idea before I took over."

Masters' mouth firmed into a stubborn line. "Yes, but if they'd known I was trying to sell they would have suffered unnecessary anxiety about their job security." He lifted his chin, an aging patriarch protecting his children from harm. "I wanted the details ironed out first."

Stephen kept his grimace in check, wondering how much nannying he'd have to do before his staff adjusted to the new professional boundaries he planned to institute. He'd agreed to keep them on, not to hold their hands and coddle them while they worked through their insecurities. "When's the meeting?"

"Three p.m. in the Da Vinci Room."

Stephen reached for the stack of manila personnel files and opened the top folder. "Doesn't give me much time to prepare," he said, glancing down at the small picture and overview of his housekeeping manager.

"Yes, but I'll help," Masters offered as he rose and then circled the desk to peer over Stephen's shoulder.

Traditionally, Stephen preferred to orient himself to the staff on his own. But he suspected the gossipy Masters wanted the opportunity to confide additional details about the staff he was handing over. And, since Stephen had discovered early on that knowing his employees' names and snippets of personal detail from their lives smoothed the transition of ownership more than anything else he could do, he resigned himself to accommodating Master as he sang his swan song.

Besides, at the end of the day, it was all about efficiency.

Efficiency, profits, and besting the competition.

A lifetime spent within the cutthroat Whitfield empire might not have provided much in the way of familial support and approval, but it *had* taught him how to run a hotel. Somehow he knew that if he resisted Masters, the transition would be delayed.

So he flipped through the pages of housekeeping employees while Masters offered commentary on each, noting who'd been in service the longest, who were the newest hires, who had children in college, spouses struggling with cancer, or had just given birth to new babies. And then they moved on to the pastry shop, restaurant and dining staff. Halfway through, Stephen's entire body froze as stunned recognition winnowed through him.

"Colette Huntington. Now *there's* a pastry chef you won't regret having on staff," said Masters, sounding like a proud patriarch touting the accomplishment of a favored daughter. "You give that girl a bit of butter, cream and flour, and she can work magic. No lie. I credit her desserts with half our return business."

"Yes," he murmured, while struggling to keep his reaction in check. "Good chefs will do that."

"Colette's not just a good chef. She's smart, hardworking, and the staff adores her."

Deep down, Stephen supposed he'd always suspected he'd run into her again. There were only so many hotels, so many decent pastry chefs, in the world. They were bound to intersect at some point. But he was careful to register none of his shock, cocking a head toward her file as if she were just another random name in the pile. "How long has she been with the Renaissance?"

"Going on four years now. She trained at Cordon Bleu, but had a devil of a time finding a job overseas."

Is that what she told you? A rush of annoyance, tinged with an odd twinge of smarting pride, cinched low in his gut. "You hired her without experience?"

"I saw her potential and took a risk. Turned out to be one of the best decisions I made." He leaned to squint fondly at her photo and shook his head. "Even though things didn't work out for her in London, poor girl, her heartbreak was definitely our gain."

Heartbreak?

"You'll like her," Masters continued as he straightened. "Everyone does. And the best part is she doesn't engage in the typical drama of a service industry. She's private, reliable, and loyal to a fault."

Hearing her described in such glowing terms, terms he might have once used himself, dredged up memories he'd discarded years ago. Memories he'd buried beneath layers of regret, resentment, and wounded pride. Memories he had no interest in revisiting. He didn't want to think about her. She didn't deserve another minute of his mental energies. She'd made a fool of him, made him *feel* when he'd vowed to avoid emotional connections. And then she'd left him.

Even so, Stephen couldn't restrain the beat of curiosity that made his muscles tense and quickened his pulse. He leaned forward to scan her file, and his focus caught on the grainy colored photo at its upper left corner. She didn't look much different than she had in London, despite the poor quality of the copy. She still had the same hazel eyes, honey-blond hair and fresh, freckled face. His fingers itched to trace the soft lines of her image, as if to recall the texture of her skin and hair, and he knotted his hand into a fist, irritated with his reaction. "She's married, I take it?"

Masters' face pleated in a grin. "Why? You interested?"

"Of course not," he answered while he forced his hand to relax atop his thigh. He was over her. Had been for a long time. "It just helps to know who might be dating within the ranks."

"Oh, Colette's not like that. She never mixes business and pleasure."

Except she had. With him. "Tell me about this Henri person," Stephen said, flipping to the next file in an attempt to put Colette out of his mind. He had no interest in ferreting out her secrets anymore. She was merely one of the employees he'd acquired in a business transaction. End of story.

She no longer had the power to affect him. To make him soft and maudlin and weak.

No one did.

"Henri's a comanager with Colette. French. Dramatic and a little emotional at times, but very, very good. He and Colette oversee all the dessert production for the Renaissance, and manage Doux Rêves during its operating hours," said Masters. "You have to be careful with Henri, though," he warned. "He likes to believe everything is his idea. Colette's the only one who can make him feel like he's in charge while implementing ideas he didn't generate."

"Is that so?" Stephen asked in a cool voice.

"Yes. Colette's a genius at navigating his moods, so if you need to make changes to Doux Rêves or the dessert menus, she's the one I'd talk to first. Get her on your side, and Henri will follow without complaint. Force any changes on Henri without Colette easing the way ahead of you, and you could have a nightmare on your hands." Masters clucked his tongue while shaking his big, gray head. "And, let me tell you, a French chef in a bad mood is impossible to work with."

"I know how to handle bad moods," Stephen said dryly. Decades of battle with a family who hated him had honed his negotiating skills to a razor-sharp edge. He had no trouble determining an opponent's greatest weakness and then exploiting it if it meant the bottom line benefited. And, since any hotel's success hinged on a seamless integration of comfort, service and quality food, he'd gain Colette's support whether she wished to grant it or not.

He wouldn't allow their shared history to compromise his investment. She'd be on board by week's end or there'd be hell to pay.

* * *

"Thank you so much for coming out on your day off," Colette said as she slipped on wedge sandals, adjusted the skirt of her emerald sleeveless dress, and then slung her purse over her shoulder. "My boss doesn't call meetings very often, but when he does, I have to attend."

"I understand, and it's no problem." Janet, a sweet woman in her sixties who'd nannied Emma from birth, scanned the kitchen for her young charge. "Where is the little scamp, anyway?"

"Changing her clothes." Colette's mouth hitched in a half-smile as they exchanged a commiserating glance. "Again."

"Janet!" squealed four-year-old Emma as she galloped into the kitchen to give her nanny a hug. "You're here!"

"I sure am, honey." Janet pressed Emma back and scanned her newest wardrobe change. "My, aren't you looking pretty this afternoon?" she observed, beaming at Emma's colorful combination of glittery princess attire and pink tennis shoes.

Emma grinned back, reaching to adjust her plastic tiara. "An' I'm wearing a crown, too."

"I see. Are you Snow White today?" Janet teased as she reached to ruffle Emma's golden girls. "Or the Little Mermaid?"

"I'm Cinderella, silly!" Emma cocked her head and then lifted her tulle skirt out from her sides. "See? My dress is blue!"

"Land's sake alive, you're right," confessed Janet in feigned chagrin as she bent to squint at Emma's dress. "It's a good thing I've got such a smart girl to remind me of my colors!"

Colette's heart pinched as she watched her daughter giggle and then spin an artless Cinderella twirl. Emma was growing up so fast that missing even one additional minute of her precious childhood made Colette wish anew for a fairy godmother of her own. Not that she'd entertain thoughts of fairytale endings ever again. Not when duty and employment and reality called.

"Come here, sweetheart," Colette said as she squatted down and hauled Emma into a hug. "Momma has a meeting at work, but I'll be done before you know it, and then we'll go to the park, okay?"

"'Kay," said Emma as she squirmed free and skipped back to Janet's side. "Love you!"

Thirty five minutes and two frenetic subway transfers later, Emma checked her watch as she pressed against the interminably slow revolving door of the Renaissance Hotel. The meeting had started four minutes ago and she hated being late.

When she neared the open convention room doors, she could hear Bill Masters' sonorous voice filling the room with its typical warmth and enthusiasm. Spotting her best friend Henri, she ducked into the chair he'd saved her in one of the back rows. "Hey," she whispered. "Did I miss anything?"

"Oui," he whispered back, his eyes wide and his face pale. "Very big news you miss. *Énorme.*"

A frisson of alarm sent ice down her spine. "What is it?"

He shushed her with a wave of his narrow hand.

"Tell me!"

Henri tipped his head toward hers and hissed, "Bill, he has sold the hotel."

She blanched, the thought of being laid off settling hard in her belly. She couldn't afford to lose her seniority, her position as manager, and start all over again. "What? Why?"

Henri pressed his lips together, confusion and worry evident in his brown eyes as he gestured toward the stage with his gelled ruff of platinum hair. "The new boss, he's bought the Renaissance already. He takes charge tomorrow."

Colette shifted her attention to the stage, tuning in to the tail-end of Bill's introduction. The man who'd been like a father to them all these past few years said something about their jobs being secure and how he'd chosen his replacement based on what was best for the Renaissance family.

"But why didn't Bill tell us anything about this?" she whispered, while the other employees surged to their feet and their questions began to crescendo. "Why keep it a secret until now?"

"Quiet down. Quiet down, folks," said Bill, leaning over the microphone with his palms extended. "Things will be fine. I promise." He dipped his attention to the front row and beckoned someone forward. "Why don't you come up here and introduce yourself?" he asked. "Set everyone's worries at ease."

The murmurs increased in volume as Colette stood as well. The employees in front of her craned their necks and rose up on tiptoes, blocking her view. Dipping to peer through a crosshatch of arms, necks and heads, she caught disjointed glimpses of their new boss as he made his way across the small stage: jet-black hair, broad shoulders, a dark hint of stubble along a chiseled plane of whiskered cheek and bone—

Her stomach reacted first, quivering with an alertness she hadn't felt for years.

No.

A dual rush of ice and fire pebbled her skin. Oh, God. She knew that profile. She knew that full, sardonic curve of lip and sharp blade of nose. She knew. Oh, God, she knew. Recognition slammed hard against her chest as Stephen Whitfield, the only man she'd ever loved, the father of her child and the millionaire who'd stolen her breath as easily as he'd claimed her virginity, stepped up to the microphone and addressed his shocked audience.

"Thank you, Masters, for your comprehensive overview of the coming transition, and thank you, Renaissance employees, for agreeing to meet with me today." He smiled, a stunning flash of white teeth, while his newest batch of employees quieted to a stunned silence. At six foot four, and dressed in an immaculate navy silk suit, Stephen oozed confident command and tempered sexuality from every pore. It was no wonder they all gaped at him like he was a pagan hunter brought in from the wild.

"Please," he said, as effortlessly comfortable before a crowd as he'd always been. "Be seated."

This had to be some sort of a dream.

He couldn't be here. He was supposed to be in London. *London.*

Stephen scanned the audience with his encouraging smile while Colette, unable to move, remained frozen in place until his gaze caught hers and held. For a breathless moment in time the world halted on its axis, the abrupt shift from present to past jarring her heartbeat into stillness.

"I realize this may come as a bit of a shock," he said without breaking eye contact. "But I want to reassure you all that for now, at least, your positions are secure." His voice, that same deep voice that had haunted her dreams since she'd fled London, left no room for doubt in her quailing heart.

He was real. Very, very real.

"Your job descriptions might change a bit," he continued, "but Masters has assured me that you are each valuable employees who will be willing to meet me halfway. Unless you prove otherwise, you can expect to remain on the payroll indefinitely."

Stephen was in New York. *Here.* The world launched back into its dizzy, perilous spin, sending rivulets of shock through her veins.

"In return for this job security, however, I will expect flexibility and loyalty from each of you." Demanding and fierce, his brutal slash of mouth, high cheekbones and icy blue eyes bore mute testimony to his insistence on making his own rules and exacting obedience from all within his realm. Thick hair the color of onyx and an angular jaw that appeared to be hewn from granite intensified his aura of power. Only his eyelashes, curling and long enough to tangle at the edges, lent any hint of softness to his commanding expression. "You best know now that I will not tolerate dissention within the ranks."

Dissention within the ranks? Her reawakening pulse ricocheted through every disbelieving cell, while his grim expression, intense and hard where before it had been warm, made icy fear clutch within her chest.

"I am willing to listen to your concerns and consider your input, but I advise you to prepare yourselves for change. The Renaissance must be brought back into profitability if it is to survive the next decade. We will have to work together to make updates in a timely fashion. If we do not, Masters' legacy will fail."

A corner of her brain registered that Henri had tugged on her arm, trying to reclaim her attention. But she remained ensnared in the web of Stephen's gaze, unable to move while he continued.

"Toward that end, I will maintain an open door policy so that we can build a working relationship as we move forward together."

She needed to escape. Now. Except with Emma in tow where would she go? Her stomach seized in denial, her throat closed up, and a tremor claimed her hands.

His eyes narrowed to slits of glinting blue. "Do you have a question?" he asked her, an edge of ice underlying the velvet smoothness of his tone.

A murmur of curiosity rippled through the seated staff and they turned as one to stare at Colette. Suddenly aware that she was still standing, she dropped like a guillotine into her chair, her limbs too numb to check her descent.

"Colette?" whispered Henri as he gripped her forearm. His warm brown eyes darkened with concern. "What is it? You are pale as *un fantôme*."

"I'm fine," she managed to say. Her pulse careened as her thoughts raced frantically. Did Stephen know about Emma yet? Did he suspect the truth? Bill was such a gossip, he'd probably told Stephen about her status as a single mother. What if Stephen tried to take Emma away? Feeling trapped, she closed her eyes and hauled in a steadying breath. Panicking wouldn't help anything. She had to be calm. She had to *think*.

Maybe she was overreacting. Stephen wasn't the type to be interested in his staff's lives outside of work. He might not have even recognized her across the crowded conference room. She wore her hair up now. Motherhood, sleepless nights and worry had stripped her of her youthful blush. And it had been five years since he'd seen her.

Besides, even if he had learned about Emma, he had no reason to suspect she was his daughter. They'd used protection every time without fail. He'd seen to that. He'd made it very, very clear that he never intended to have children.

She didn't need to worry, she told herself while struggling to calm her thudding pulse.

He wouldn't want her again. And he certainly wouldn't want Emma.

Wasn't that why she'd left in the first place?

The rest of the meeting passed in a blur. Stephen's speech, outlining the schedule of pending renovations and his vision for the future of the Renaissance, barely penetrated the turmoil of her thoughts. But when he announced the schedule for supervisor meetings the following day, her panic kicked back into gear.

"I'll meet with the lobby supervisors at eight a.m." he said, "followed by housekeeping at nine, Doux Rêves and dessert management at ten, guest services at eleven, maintenance at noon, and La Tour d'Or management at one. If you cannot attend for any reason, please notify me as soon as possible so that I can make alternative arrangements." He closed his binder and scanned his seated employees a final time before thanking Bill and adjourning the meeting.

Everyone stood to leave, their low murmurs rising like

the hum of bees moving to a new hive. Colette joined them, grappling with her reaction to his announcement regarding personal meetings. Blending in with an anonymous crowd of employees was doable. But maintaining her poise in a face-to-face interview would prove far more difficult, especially when she didn't know how much he knew.

"Do you think he'd want to renovate *me*?" whispered one of the new girls from the front desk as they congregated in the aisle.

"If you're lucky," giggled her friend as she fanned her face and stole another covert look over her shoulder. "Did you see his eyes?"

"Eyes?" commiserated yet another. "I was too busy fantasizing about those shoulders, that hair, and those big, strong hands." Two of the students shared a joint sigh of agreement while the third girl continued, "Can you imagine how a specimen like that would perform in bed?"

"Tiffany!" they scolded with shocked gasps of titillation. "What if he hears you? He's our new *boss*!"

The pretty coed didn't even blush. "So? I'd be happy to trade in my position for one that's a little more…unprofessional with a man who looks like that. Wouldn't you?"

Colette ducked her head, feeling her own face heat. She'd thought the same thing when she wasn't much older than these girls. And she'd paid the price for her foolishness.

If she were a better person, she'd warn the girls away from him before they got hurt.

But they wouldn't listen. Why would they? She certainly hadn't.

She'd nearly reached the exit when the gossip around her decreased in volume. An air of expectancy rushed to fill the silence and the fine hairs on Colette's arms rose.

"Miss Huntington," Stephen called. The edge of command carried the same immutable force of will as it had five years ago. "A moment, please."

Stumbling forward as if she hadn't heard, she continued toward the door without glancing back.

The shock of Stephen's warm fingers at her elbow, recognizable even after all this time, sent a shiver of awareness coursing through her veins. Awareness she couldn't afford to feel, yet felt all the same.

"Miss Huntington," he repeated, more sharply this time.

Fear, hot and sharp and irrational, leaked from her lungs into her muscles and nerves and skin. Fighting the fear, she lifted her chin and turned to face him as if his touch impacted her not at all. "I'm sorry?"

His eyes narrowed, whether in amusement or anger she couldn't tell. "I wish to speak with you."

Feigning surprise, she lifted both brows. "Now?"

A wintry smile that didn't quite reach his eyes revealed a flash of white teeth. "Yes."

She felt the weight of her coworkers' regard, sensed the murmur of gossip they'd leave in their wake. "Why?"

"Perhaps we should adjourn to my new office to discuss it."

Panic raced down her spine, but she forced a bland note of polite courtesy to her voice. "I'd be happy to oblige you any other day, Mr. Whitfield. Today, however, I have a prior commitment."

Her curious colleagues stalled in their mass exodus, their ears and eyes trained on the merest hint of scandal involving their new boss. Stephen raised his gaze to his nosy employees, his expression exuding an unmistakable authority. "Is there a problem?" he intoned, and the subtext of his words couldn't have been more clear.

Dismissed with nothing more than a polite question, her coworkers jumped as if they'd been jolted with a cattle prod. Within seconds the double doors of the conference room had

clicked closed and Stephen and she were plunged into muffled silence. The pulse rushing in her ears formed the only
sound, her serrated breath its only counterpoint.

CHAPTER THREE

STEPHEN'S nostrils flared, though his smile remained fixed in place. "Now, what was it you were saying about a previous commitment?"

Colette swallowed nervously and avoided his eyes. "I said I couldn't stay today. I have an appointment."

Still tall and broad, he wore his power as easily as his designer suit. The inscrutable expression he wore possessed the same seductive persuasiveness it always had. "Cancel it."

"I can't."

"Of course you can. Anything can be rescheduled."

"True," she improvised, unwilling to renege on her promise to Emma. "But I'd prefer not to."

When he didn't respond, she raised her eyes to his, only to find his blue gaze glinting with challenge. "Is this really how you wish to play it?"

She felt her neck tighten defensively. "Play it?"

"Colette," he scolded with a patronizing smile. "You know me. I know you. And you're far too intelligent to think I'm interested in these games."

Up close, he was even more beautiful than she remembered. Except, like a faded photograph that had been brought out into the light too many times, her memory of him was softer. More gentle. Now he looked inaccessible in a way he hadn't before. Strong, remote and polished. He made her wonder if any of his grim smiles ever contained the warmth of her memories.

"It's not a game. This is my only day off, and my schedule is impossibly tight." She made a show of checking her watch. "I'm late as it is."

"Then meet me after you're done." The quiet command, delivered in a low, dangerous hum, resonated through her body, reminding her of the way he'd dismantled every barrier she'd ever thrown up. No wall, no door would ever keep Stephen Whitfield out. Once he saw something he wanted, he went after it with a single minded purpose no defenses could protect against. Surrender, no matter how short-lived, was guaranteed.

"No," she blurted, withdrawing from the heat of his nearness until her heels bumped against the closed door. "We already have an appointment tomorrow morning. I'm sure anything we have to discuss can wait until then."

He arched a brow. "There are a few items in your personnel file we need to address. Items I'm sure you don't want Henri to hear."

A fresh wave of panic flooded her chest. Had Bill written something in her file about Emma? "What items?"

"Your file indicates that you've been here for four years."

"Yes," she hedged, studying his eyes for any hint of what he already knew. "So?"

"So where were you for the year between London and here?"

I was having your child. "Does it matter?"

"Why don't you let me be the judge of what matters and what doesn't?"

She inhaled as she cast about for reasonable excuses, knowing she navigated a fine boundary between placating him and raising his suspicions. "The job market was tight when I first returned. It took me a while to find a position that fit my skills." *And my childcare schedule.*

"Perhaps you should have asked me for a reference."

She let the statement pass without comment.

His gaze flicked over her body, managing to be both dismissive and unnerving at the same time. "How did you manage to acquire the Renaissance position without any documented work history?"

"Who knows?" She shrugged. Licked her suddenly dry lips. "Perseverance? Luck? Pounding the pavement for long enough that Masters took pity on me?"

Narrowing his eyes in speculative assessment, he flattened his mouth into a grim line. "Right. Masters *pitied* you enough to hire you despite your apparent lack of experience." He paused, the accusation beneath his words as clear as if he'd spoken it aloud. "Why do you suppose that was?"

Defensive without having any reason to be, she hitched her chin. "Why don't you ask him?"

"I did," Stephen admitted smoothly. "He claims he took a chance on you. A chance he seems to be quite proud of taking."

"Well, it has nothing to do with what you're thinking," she insisted. "He just likes to support the locals."

"The locals?"

Uncomfortable with her slip, she bit back a silent curse. "Yes."

"Since when are you local?"

She exhaled noisily through her nostrils. "Since I was born."

His brow hitched high. "How did I not know that?"

There's a lot you don't know.

When she didn't answer, he moved closer, crowding into her space and forcing her to tip her head back to maintain eye contact. "You never did tell me much about your past, did you?"

She felt her body flush hot and then cold. "No, I didn't, and I'd like to keep it that way."

Challenge flashed in his expression, firming his mouth and making his jaw bunch. "I'm not surprised. And I suppose you'd like to pretend we don't know each other as well, right? Pretend to be strangers when we're anything but?"

"Of course," she blurted, grappling for a tone of normalcy despite her racing pulse. "It's been five years. We've lived on different continents, led separate lives. I think it's safe to assume we've both moved on."

"And yet here we are. Together again."

"We aren't *together*," she corrected with a thin, brittle voice, while both hands wrapped tightly around the strap of her purse. "We're simply boss and employee. Nothing more. I don't see any reason to acknowledge we have any history together at all."

His gaze flicked to her knotted hands and strained expression before he leaned even closer. Close enough for the safe distance she'd shored up between her heart and the pain of leaving him to vanish in an unwelcome surge of heat. "So you're...comfortable...pretending we never had an affair?"

Too unnerved to form a reply, she simply stared up at his achingly beautiful features, trying to make sense of his sudden reappearance in her life. Why wasn't he in London? At the Whitfield Grand where he belonged? "Of course," she finally managed. "Our...involvement...is hardly something I've been proud of, and hauling it out for inspection now, five years after the fact, will only complicate matters for everyone."

His expression, as hard and inscrutable as granite, didn't change as he stared at her for a long, tense moment. "For everyone? Or just for you?"

A flash of pique washed over her, sharpening her tone. "I was the subject of malicious hotel gossip because of our... whatever it was we had, and I've no desire to repeat the experience. I'd ask that you respect my decision to keep my personal life private this time around."

"*This* time? I'd say privacy is a permanent state for you, Colette." The sultry pitch of his voice called up memories she'd spent the last five years trying to eradicate. It made her skin buzz with awareness and brought a terrifying weakness to her knees. His gaze dipped to her mouth, her throat, the scalloped neckline of her dress. "It took me months to excavate even the tiniest crack in that shell of yours."

Heat burned a fiery path from chest to hairline, and Colette swallowed in an attempt to regain her composure, to quell her body's response to his nearness. "Yes, well, I let my guard down with you when I shouldn't have," she said, clearing her throat. "What we shared was…temporary. We were on a fast track to nowhere. You knew it as well as I."

His eyes reclaimed hers. "While you made sure we had no detours along the way, didn't you?"

She hated the accusation in his tone, the unwelcome sting of guilt his words wrought. "Why are you even here, Stephen? You own the Whitfield Grand, and a place like that doesn't run itself."

His mouth tipped into a cold, grim curve. "Did I imply it did?"

"You're not there. What else am I supposed to think?"

"I only own fifty percent of the Grand. And ever since the family's economic downturn, several other partial owners have taken a renewed interest in its day-to-day operations." His nostrils flared with palpable annoyance. "I find I don't like sharing the wheel."

She stared at him in surprise, unable to envision the Whitfield Grand with anyone but Stephen at the helm. "Surely they'd want you to remain in charge, given how successfully you ran it before?"

"You'd think so, but you'd be wrong." His controlled expression only hinted at his carefully corralled temper. "The Whitfields and I don't see eye to eye on a lot of things and it's proven…interesting, to say the least. Fortunately I've spent the past few years expanding my holdings beyond the Grand, and I've been able to disengage on occasion."

"But why New York?" she asked. "I'd have thought you'd be quite content dominating Europe."

"Don't be modest," he said. "You know my interest in America all began with you."

She flushed and dropped her gaze to the knot of his maroon tie. "Don't be absurd."

"I'm not," he said, with the same whiskey heat of their past, firing her blood with a disconcerting blend of fear and awareness.

She clung to the fear, determined to dispel the memory of his voice caressing her in the dark.

"You didn't even know I was in New York," she reminded him as she raised her eyes. "I had nothing to do with your decision to buy the Renaissance."

A small, triumphant smile crooked his mouth, straying nowhere near his eyes. "Then I guess fate has intervened, hasn't it?"

"I don't believe in fate."

He cocked his head, his gaze flashing with heat before a sweep of dark lashes shuttered his response from view. "You haven't changed at all, have you? You're still stubborn. Still secretive. Still confident that you can control everything."

"There's nothing wrong with being in charge of my own life."

"You can't control the world. Other lives will intercept yours whether you want them to or not."

"Not if I don't allow it," she insisted, scuttling sideways. Away from him.

"I see you're still good at pushing people away." He tracked her retreat, robbing her of her equilibrium and the false sense of security her space provided.

She firmed her jaw. "Yes."

"I wonder how long it's going to take for you to figure out that I always push back."

Facing the only man with whom she'd ever lowered her guard, the only man who'd been persistent enough to chip through her walls, she marshaled her defenses anew. She couldn't allow him to drag her into a discussion of their past. Too much was at stake. "You kept me here to talk about my file," she reminded him. "So, unless there's something else you need to discuss, I really am expected elsewhere."

His intent blue gaze told her he wasn't to be diverted. "What did you tell Masters about your time in London?"

She scowled, trying desperately to ignore the little flip in her stomach his question elicited. "Why were you discussing me with Bill?"

"I wasn't. He volunteered things without a single query from me."

Sucking in a shallow breath, she squared her shoulders and prepared for the worst. "Bill talks too much."

"He gave me the distinct impression that you'd been *wounded* in London. He intimated that you were skittish, single, and still smarting from an emotional hit you'd suffered overseas."

She was going to throttle Bill the next time she saw him. "He tried to set me up with his grandson a couple of times," she said, lifting her chin as she kept her expression unruffled and calm. "When I refused, he must have assumed the worst."

Black lashes drifted over his probing blue gaze. "Assumptions are the damnedest things, aren't they?"

She steeled her features and stared at him without blinking. She didn't dare catalog the simmering intensity of his question, didn't dare acknowledge the climbing heat in her veins. "Do you have a point?"

A smile, lazy and far too seductive, tipped to claim one side of his mouth. "I always have a point."

"Then please make it so I can leave."

"Right. I forgot." He tossed her an enigmatic look. "Things get a little uncomfortable, a little personal, and rather than face it you run."

"I don't *run*," she protested, while nervousness beat against her throat. "I leave. There's a difference."

"Then explain it to me." He moved to bracket her shoulders between his powerful braced arms. "Explain how dropping everything—your job, your life and your lover—and disappearing across the Atlantic without a word to anyone isn't running."

"I didn't leave without a word," she said, while panic coiled low in her gut. He was too close. Too big and imposing and distracting. "I told you I wanted out. And you said you understood."

"You also agreed to wait until I returned from Paris."

She stared at him in desperate, defiant silence, refusing him the explanation she couldn't risk giving.

He dipped his mouth even closer and murmured, "Explain why, if you weren't running, you couldn't wait two weeks for me to come back."

Awareness winnowed through her, bringing a flush of heat to her face, her neck, her breasts. "Maybe I just decided there were more important things to do than while away the hours in bed with a man," she said.

He obviously didn't believe her, and the knowing glint of fire in his blue eyes made a reciprocal flare of heat coil deep in her belly. "Used to be you couldn't spend enough time in my bed," he reminded her.

"Yes, well, I was young and foolish," she insisted. "I've grown up since then."

"Tell me." His tone, laced with sarcasm and a hint of bite, told her she'd insulted him. "What precipitated this amazing foray into maturity?"

Becoming a mother to your daughter.

His gaze trapped hers and the silence stretched out between them, a palpable weight in the air. "Did I *wound* you, Colette?" he taunted.

Her chest felt tight and a knot of pain she'd thought long buried thickened her throat. "Of course not. I'm the one who left, remember?"

"Yes, I do remember," he said, and his focus tracked the line of her neck before returning to her face. "It's you who wants to forget."

She shifted from beneath his accusatory gaze, pressing back against the sturdy support of the door. "Do you blame me?"

"You realize, don't you, that memories of our passion will intrude whether we wish it or not?" His eyes, heated and heavy lidded, dipped to her mouth. "All those nights and days and hours spent worshiping each other's bodies won't just disappear because we want them to."

She licked her lips while her pulse gathered speed in her chest, her belly, her hands. "It doesn't mean I have to acknowledge them."

"You think?" he asked as his fingers slowly rose to graze her brow. "Because when I saw your file and realized we'd be working together again, I was worried. Worried about how you'd respond once you realized I was here. And the necessity of keeping things on a professional footing became undeniably clear."

She swallowed, the glancing touch of his fingertips against her bare skin sending a shiver along her spine. "There's no need to worry. I can keep things professional."

"But I didn't know that, did I? That's why we needed to speak privately." He stared at her from beneath hooded eyes. "Without the other employees overhearing. I needed to set the parameters of how we'd act together so there'd be no confusion."

She maintained a tenuous hold on her composure. "I'm not confused."

"Good." His thumb grazed the sensitive transition from brow to cheek. "Because I can't afford for our past to interfere with the plans I have for the Renaissance and its future."

Flames licked low in her belly and her mouth felt perilously dry. "I know," she said, praying she spoke the truth. "It won't."

"Even when we're in your kitchen together?" he asked. His blue gaze challenged her to deny the memories of all the conversations they'd shared while she baked for him, all the times they'd explored each other's bodies with wild, passionate abandon. "Or when I'm sampling your creations before they're added to the menu?

"You already know my recipes," she rushed to reassure him, lifting her face from his touch. "And the dessert menus are set."

A single black brow questioned her assertion. "You've created nothing new in the five years we've been apart?"

Besides a beautiful child you know nothing about? "I've been too busy with the management side of my job."

"That's disappointing." Heat gathered behind the blue of his eyes. "I was looking forward to learning another recipe or two."

As if she'd dare to teach him again. She'd taught him every unique blend of spice, liqueur, and specialty flour she knew. She'd taught him to measure with his hands, to see with his mouth and tongue and to taste with his nose and eyes and skin. Their culinary lessons had invariably involved far, far more than mere food. Her flesh heated at the memory and she ducked her head to hide her blush.

He tilted her face back up again with one fingertip, the seductive curve of his mouth saying far more than any words he might have uttered.

"I wouldn't teach you regardless," she said, clearing her

throat and forcing the memories aside. "It wouldn't be a good idea for either of us."

"Yes. I suppose it's better to keep things impersonal," he said he tracked the damning evidence of her blush, that single point of contact between them radiating out to every cell.

"Definitely," she said, hating how her body craved his touch, how it rebelled at the thought of never being with him again. She wanted to maintain her distance, to keep Emma safe. So why this inconvenient yearning to connect with him as she had once before? To dissect every minute of the past five years they'd spent apart? To learn all the secrets of his past that she'd never had the courage to uncover?

Inhaling against the urge to press for details she had no business knowing, she lifted her chin and said, "You're right about the Renaissance. It's struggling. We all need to be focused if we're going to turn it around. We can't afford any distractions or rumors."

"I couldn't agree more." His voice, smooth as silk, jarred her with its undertones of controlled, tempered steel.

Though he appeared to be relaxed, something was dangerously off. She could feel it humming in the air between them, making her skin prick with awareness.

She swallowed noisily and tried to muster a smile. It felt horribly forced and strained. "Well, then, I'm glad we got that cleared up."

"As am I."

She dropped her gaze to her watch, lifting her wrist between them. "I really need to go."

"This appointment of yours...is it personal?" The question, delivered in a light, conversational tone, felt like a test. A test she had no chance of passing.

"Does it matter?" she asked in a thin voice.

"Unfortunately..." he began. His unrelenting focus trapped hers, and then he slowly lifted his palm to her cheek and stared down at her before saying, "I find it does."

"But it can't," she answered on a thready exhale. "We agreed to keep things professional."

"You're right," he said with a sardonic smile. "But our bodies don't seem to be listening, do they?"

"Mine is," she lied, while the seductive warmth of his hand sent a current of longing down her limbs. She wanted to bolt, to lurch away from his commanding touch, but her brain's ability to control her muscles seemed to have shut down.

His eyes dipped to her traitorous body, taking in the flush of her skin, the agitated rise and fall of her breasts, and then returned. "Liar."

She trembled with her denial. "I'm not lying," she whispered. "I don't want this."

"Prove it."

Unable to speak, she sucked in an unsteady thread of breath while his thumb tracked back and forth along her sensitive lower lip.

"What if this is just fate's way of dealing with the past we never resolved?" he asked. "What if I was meant to find you again? To pick up where we left off?"

"I told you. I don't believe in fate." A sharp flare of desire shot through her belly as he abandoned her mouth to align both hands along the sides of her jaw. Immobile, her heart clamoring against her ribs, she remained frozen as she felt the imprint of his fingers along her flesh.

"I miss seeing your hair down," he told her. "Do you remember how you used to wear it loose around your shoulders and down your back?"

Yes, she remembered. She remembered the way he'd buried his hands in its length, pulling her head back to expose her throat to his mouth. She remembered the way he'd drawn strands of it over his lips, tasting her scent while he stared deep into her eyes. She remembered, too, the way it had fallen like a rippled curtain of candlelit gold over the two of them while she rode them both to completion.

Before she realized his intention his hands moved, his wide palms skimming her ear and nape as he released her giant hairclamp in one smooth, efficient move.

Her hair tumbled down her back in a single coil and she immediately reached to repair the damage. But before she could lift the heavy mass from her nape his hands stalled hers.

"Don't," he murmured. His fingers tunneled through the mass of her hair, spreading the curls over her shoulders. "Do you know I still dream about your hair?"

The low rasp of his voice, soft as velvet, made her tremble. He must have detected the subtle shiver along her flesh because his grip tightened against her shoulders and he dragged her closer. As much as she wanted to pull free, another part of her responded to the demanding strength of his touch, to the command underscoring his nearness.

Lifting her hands to push him away, she froze when her fingertips touched the warm thickness of his wrists. Her thumbs pressed against the channel of tendons at the base of his palms while her fingertips involuntarily recalled the hard landscape of bones and flesh in his forearm. She heard his swift intake of breath, watched his chest expand and rise, and her hands refused to abandon his smooth, hair-dusted skin. Time stretched, grew taut, while the silence beat between them.

His head sank lower, until she felt the heat of his breath against her neck. "Colette—"

Dismayed by her irrational response to his nearness, she pressed him back, releasing his wrists and breaking the tenuous contact. "No," she told him, retreating a sideways step. "We can't do this."

"Why not?"

Confusion warred with her need to escape. Now.

"Tell me you feel it, too." He followed her, his low voice

urging her to reconsider. To relent. "Tell me you remember how good it was between us."

Hypnotized by the fiery intensity of his blue eyes, she knotted her fists at her sides and swallowed. He didn't move again, simply waiting in silence while she battled her desire to touch him again. "It doesn't matter. We're over."

His mouth pressed into a sober line, lending a grimness to the perfection of his face. "Are we?" he asked quietly.

Before she had a chance to prepare herself, his warm palms cupped her face and tilted her mouth toward his. Her startled inhale did nothing to deter him, and his dark head dipped toward hers with unerring accuracy. Her fingers flew to his forearms even as the muscled wall of his chest bumped her breasts, pressing her against the closed door while his mouth covered hers. The fiery, voracious, delicious assault of his lips stunned her. Consumed her.

An incendiary blaze of sensation tore through her and her hands tightened at his wrists, floundering between the urge to shove him back or pull him closer. He made the decision for her, releasing her head and dragging her up against the granite cove of his body. Curving over her, he possessed her within the hard circle of his arms, the wide arc of his shoulders and chest. She felt secure…desired…needed. All the things she'd always felt with Stephen. All the things she knew could never be trusted. It was all happening so fast. Too fast. She inhaled raggedly through her nose, filling her senses with a combination of crisp cotton, cedarwood, and the clean bite of his soap.

His mouth released hers and then withdrew, to create a hair's breadth between them. He hauled in a deep breath and then exhaled, wafting mint-scented warmth over her trembling lips. She felt the bump of his nose against hers, and then the glancing brush of his mouth against her temple while the splayed fingers of his hands against her back and shoulderblades kept her from sinking to the floor in a boneless heap.

Stephen had always kissed her this way, hauling her close enough to sample her flesh with his lips and tongue, tasting her as if she were a banquet and he a starving man. It made it difficult to remember that being with him was a risk she couldn't afford to take.

"I think you should go now," he whispered, leaning close to her ear. "You don't want to be late."

CHAPTER FOUR

STEPHEN waited for several long, torturous moments after she'd left the conference room, struggling to control his breathing and the flare of arousal that had caught him so completely off guard.

What the hell was he doing?

Just as he had the first time he'd seen her, he'd reacted without thought to the consequences, rushing into the firestorm that was Colette without regard for the fact that he'd get burned.

He'd done the same thing when they'd met, when he'd dared to enter her kitchen just as she was taking a trio of soufflés out of the oven. He'd startled her, making her jump, and the soufflés had fallen before they could be served.

The new American pastry chef he'd hired sight unseen from Cordon Bleu's new crop of graduates hadn't known that he was her boss, and she'd laid into him for being a clod-footed klutz. When he'd had the audacity to apologize for his clumsiness, she'd ranted at him as if he'd skinned her favorite cat.

Amused and surprised by her outburst, he'd simply waited while she lashed him with her sharp tongue. He hadn't been able to remember the last time a woman had scolded him, and certainly not one as fierce as the hazel-eyed Colette Huntington. Her candor and her lack of fear had enthralled him, and he'd been enchanted. Intoxicated. He'd asked her out the minute she stopped to draw breath.

He still didn't understand why he'd done it. His tastes usually ran to petite females who were sweet, dulcet, and brunette. But for some reason Miss Huntington's long, lanky limbs and fierce, freckled lioness mien had piqued an interest that had lain dormant for years.

Whether his response to her was rational or not hadn't mattered. He'd liked that she wasn't one of those obsequious employees who kowtowed to his every whim and was too afraid of him to speak their mind. She'd intrigued him.

Colette had refused his request for an evening out, of course, even after he'd told her who he was.

"Why not?" he'd asked, flashing the trademark grin that always softened women into compliance. "Rumor has it I'm a pretty decent date, I can converse with the best of them, and I kiss like the very devil himself."

Her stern mouth had twitched with the barest hint of a smile. "So I've heard."

"Because you were asking about me?" he'd teased, feigning shock. "Oh, sweet, you could have come directly to the source. I'd have answered all your questions firsthand."

Her smile had bloomed, transforming her face and taking his breath away. "Not a chance," she'd answered. "I've been warned about you."

"Me?"

"You're a player," she'd said without hesitation. "And I'm to avoid you at all costs."

"You don't strike me as the type who avoids anything simply because of its reputed risk."

She'd gestured toward her deflated desserts. "Those soufflés are like the women foolish enough to succumb to your charm. They ride high on the thrill for a while, but they always end up falling. I suspect, with you, the fall comes sooner than later. So, no, thank you. I'm flattered, but no." And with that she'd turned back to her work as if he hadn't even been there.

It had taken him another three weeks to catch her in a moment's weakness and change her mind. After their first dinner together it had taken another month of wooing before he'd been allowed his first glimpse behind the walls she'd built between herself and the world. But he'd persevered.

After what had felt like decades of concerted effort, he'd finally slipped beneath her bristly resolve and unearthed her buried layers of humor and softness. He'd coaxed her into relaxing, into loosening all that lovely blond hair and laying down that arsenal of emotional weapons she'd spent a lifetime collecting.

Imagining her long, sleek body wrapped around his had fueled his patience for months. And when she'd finally, finally surrendered her virginity to him, it had been as if all his wildest fantasies had come to fruition.

The final two months of their affair had been an explosive coming together that made all his previous experiences with women pale by comparison. When she hadn't been busy crafting magic in his hotel's kitchen they'd spent every minute together, exploring each others' bodies, steeping themselves in erotic pleasure, gorging on her culinary creations and hiding away in various Whitfield properties across Europe.

And then he'd returned from Paris, determined to convince her to stay, only to find her gone. Vanished. He'd spent four days trying to contact her, leaving messages on her phone and in her email inbox. After she'd disconnected her number, he'd discovered that she'd paid her month's rent in full, packed up and left with no forwarding address.

He had never been rejected before, and her unexpected departure had stunned the hell out of him. He'd told her to wait until he came home from Paris, to give them a chance to work things out. And yet she'd left anyway.

He hadn't been prepared for the pain of it, for the searing, inescapable truth of her rejection. His family had never made any secret of their hatred for him, but he'd been able to discount their opinion. They could rot in hell for all he cared. He didn't need them. But somehow, without even realizing it, he'd come to depend on Colette and the way she made him feel.

Finding her gone and knowing he wasn't good enough for her had hurt like hell. But a couple of days later his pain had transformed to anger. Who did she think she was?

She was the one who'd made a mistake, rejecting him. He didn't need her. He'd just been momentarily blinded. He didn't need *feelings* that derailed him from the things that were important. Feelings that made him lose focus. So he'd moved on. He'd thrown himself back into work and the singles' scene without looking back.

With a different woman on his arm every weekend, he'd had no time to even think about Colette. No time to nurse his wounded pride. But lately it had felt like he was merely going through the motions. Putting on a show and keeping up appearances. Catching any woman he wanted had become too predictable. Too boring. Even the thrill of the chase had begun to pall.

Until now.

He pinched the bridge of his nose and cursed his impulsive reaction to Colette's unexpected reappearance in his life.

Had he learned nothing?

He told himself he must be some sort of masochist to pursue her again. Why couldn't he just leave well enough alone? Why couldn't he maintain the professional distance he'd claimed to want?

He tried to tell himself it was about unfinished business, about proving to her that it was *he* who held the upper hand. She was simply a loose end, a question whose answer had eluded him for far too long. Once he figured her out, determined what made her tick, he'd be able to fit her into the neat little box he'd fashioned for her and never look back again.

Yes. That was it. She was a loose end that simply needed tying up. He was satisfying his curiosity and putting the past to rest. That was all.

Confident that he'd made sense of his own reactions, he strode back toward the stage to collect his briefcase.

He'd made it only halfway when the door slammed open, startling him and drawing his attention back to the entrance of the conference room.

Colette entered on a gust of outrage and flung the door shut behind her, her freckled skin flushed a distressed apricot hue and her hazel eyes snapping with autumn fire. She stalked toward him, her fury a living, breathing entity between them, and he instinctively braced for her attack.

She stopped short of slapping him, though her fists were knotted at her thighs and her glare could have melted glass. "Don't you *ever* kiss me like that again," she ground out, her nostrils flaring with the edict. "I'm over you. Done. Finished. And I don't appreciate you acting like there's something between us when there's not."

It had been so long since she'd scolded him, it made him want to storm her defenses just to remind her that her weapons wouldn't work against him. Had she forgotten he always won? That they *both* always won? It had been too long since he'd gone head to head with Colette, too long since he'd blurred the battle lines with kisses and touches and soft murmured words.

Looking at her now, he felt the same rush of arousal he'd always felt, the same fevered need to draw her out of her shell. But he concealed his reaction with a careless shrug and a half-smile. "I'm not going to apologize for something we both wanted."

"I didn't *want* you to kiss me," she said in a sharp voice. "I don't want anything from you beyond employment. I thought I made that very clear."

He dragged his eyes away from her heaving breasts, those magnificent breasts that made him want to compose sonnets and slay dragons when he should be focused on keeping his distance. "Then why did you kiss me back?" he asked in his most reasonable tone of voice. And why did he have to fight the irrational, inconvenient urge to haul her into his arms and kiss her into soft, willing compliance again?

Her lies compressed into a firm white line as she grappled with the truth of his statement. "You caught me off guard," she finally said.

Maybe it was her wide bronze eyes, wounded and vulnerable despite her outward fire, or maybe it was the hint of worry that notched lines between her golden brows. Maybe it was the determined seam of her lush mouth, a mouth that should have been lax and curved with sensual pleasure. Whatever it was, it fired a fierce compulsion to take her to his bed and have his wicked way with her. "Maybe you caught me off guard, too."

Colette opened and then closed her mouth. It was the first time he'd seen her speechless, and it was surprisingly satisfying.

"You have to admit you were just as curious as I," he said, crossing his arms beneath his ribs and leaning back against one of the meeting chairs. "With the way we left things, it's only natural to wonder."

"I wasn't wondering," she claimed as her gaze slid away from his.

He felt the smile dent his cheek. "You always were a terrible liar."

"Fine," she admitted with an irritated flare of nostril. "We were curious and now we know. But it can't happen again. Ever. Understood?"

"Perfectly," he agreed easily.

She glared at him, her expression telegraphing an intoxicating combination of reluctant arousal and suspicion. "I don't want to speak with you about our past, I don't want to kiss you, and I certainly don't want to sleep with you again," she said, her eyes flashing with fierce heat. "Are we clear?"

"Absolutely."

"And you agree to minimize the time we spend together?"

He held her gaze for a silent beat, and then dipped his attention to her mouth and breasts for the faintest flicker of time before returning. "Don't fret, sweet. I have no plans to join you in your bed."

Color seeped into her cheeks. "Good."

Unless, of course, you beg to join me in mine.

Three short days later, after a frenzy of meetings and discussions about renovations and new directions, Colette approached Doux Rêves to find Stephen alone, awaiting her arrival. Dressed in another sleek business suit, this time in an espresso silk almost as dark as his hair, he'd foregone his typical tie. The hint of informality lent him a dangerous edge of sex appeal and made him look incongruously male against the whimsical backdrop of a French bakery.

Her steps slowed reflexively, but she firmed her resolve and forced her feet back to their initial pace. *He's just your employer now. Nothing more.* "I thought I was meeting the contractor today," she said as soon as she reached him, a frisson of nervousness making her voice come out less steady than she'd intended.

"We had an electrical emergency on the eighth floor," he said. "But I have an interior decorator I'd like you to meet instead."

Colette scanned the dark interior of the bakery and its visible slice of kitchen, finding only shadowed booths, display cases and stacks of dishes. "Where?"

He tossed her a carnal glance that made her skin bloom with heat. "My office."

"What about Henri?"

"I sent him to meet with some new dry goods suppliers to see if he could negotiate better prices."

Knowing full well that Henri would fight every design idea they generated in his absence, she said, "He won't like being left out of the discussion."

"I know. Masters told me as much. But he also told me that once you're on board you're very good at convincing him to come around. I thought we could discuss the changes I envision before Henri has a chance to argue against my suggestions."

An alliance with Stephen, no matter how innocuous it might appear on the surface, did not feel at all safe. "I'm not comfortable with the mediator role," she told him, squaring her shoulders and meeting his eyes with a confidence she didn't feel. "Not with everything else changing as much as it is."

A cocked brow challenged her concerns. "You mediated for Masters."

"Yes. But you're not Bill," she said.

"No, I'm not," Stephen said in a silky voice, ushering her forward with a gentle press of his palm against her lower spine. "Come. It won't take long at all, and then you'll be free for the remainder of the day."

She lurched forward, away from the burning heat of his touch.

"You can handle a meeting in my office, can't you?" he asked, his mouth crooked with the challenge.

"Of course," she said, feeling foolish for her reaction even as her pulse quickened against her throat. She strode toward the administrators' elevator with a brisk, professional clip. "I'm perfectly capable of carrying on a simple business conversation with you."

He matched her pace and she felt his heated gaze slide over her profile. "It's not the conversation I'm worried about. It's the location," he said with a knowing smile. "You remember, don't you, how we used to make love in my London office nearly every workday afternoon?"

"No," she snapped. "I don't." Even as she feigned immunity to his presence, her body betrayed her lie. Her skin still tingled from his innocuous touch upon her back and her breath felt perilously shallow. Not that she couldn't fake calmness with the best of them.

They continued in silence while her pulse picked up speed. Drawing in a deep breath, she braced herself for the onslaught of memories that were sure to come.

Stephen swiped his key and the wood-paneled doors of the elevator slid open silently. "After you," he said, extending his right arm.

Being careful not to touch him, she stepped into the elevator and immediately turned to face the panel of buttons. How many times had he summoned her to his office under the pretext of some business concern, only to devour her mouth and body the moment the elevator doors closed? And how many times had she welcomed him, launching herself into his arms, winding her legs about his waist, while he pleasured her against the elevator wall? Heat coursed through her at the thought, and she forced herself to remain utterly still as his hot regard against the side of her face sent awareness winnowing through her veins.

You can do this. Just don't look at him. Don't breathe.

The elevator's chime signaled their arrival and her breath escaped in a rush. Before he could say a word, or touch her, she bolted out into the new office space that he'd claimed as his own. She heard his small huff of laughter behind her before he stopped at his secretary's desk.

"Has Ms. Turner arrived yet?" he asked the older woman,

who'd dressed in serviceable tweed despite the early summer heat.

"No. She called to say she was running a few minutes late," she answered. "Shall I try to reschedule?"

"No. There's no rush," he said as he strode into the spacious office that overlooked Central Park and shut the door.

"It looks like we have a few minutes to ourselves before Ms. Turner arrives," he told her. He joined her at the window. "Can I get you something to drink while we wait?"

Colette swallowed unsteadily. The room was suddenly hot despite its subtle current of air conditioning. "No, thank you. I'm fine."

His posture tugged his taupe shirt taut against the muscled plane of his chest and it reminded her of how much taller and broader he was than she. Of how much warmer his skin had always been. "You seem a little tense," he observed.

"I'm not." Standing so close, she could smell him, and she fought the urge to simply close her eyes and inhale large draughts until her lungs filled. His scent put any delicacy she'd ever made to shame: spicy, warm, and tinged with just a hint of salt and musk, it made her want to lick him. To taste him and steep herself in all the lovely flavors of his skin. And, even as she told herself not to notice, she was excruciatingly aware of the tanned wedge of flesh at his exposed throat. How many times had she nuzzled that transition from chest to neck, tracing his beautiful, scented musculature with her lips and tongue?

"Are you sure?" he asked. His gaze crinkled with subtle amusement as he surveyed her hot face. "Because your face is a little flushed."

"I'm fine," she blurted, trying to disguise her reaction to his nearness. "I just hate wasting time."

"Because you have so many other things to do now that our kitchens are temporarily closed?" he said dryly.

She remained mutinously silent at that.

"After we meet with Ms. Turner, I'd like you to visit a few of our competitors' bakeries with me this afternoon."

"What? Why?"

His smile seemed oddly parental. "I need to determine what works and what doesn't here in New York. Since my frame of reference is European, the feedback of a local like you would prove invaluable." He pointed several blocks down to a neighboring hotel, and then shifted his gaze to hers. "I've heard Antoine's is particularly good, and I thought we'd start there first."

She bit her lip, her focus flitting from Antoine's to his expectant face and then back again. "I don't think that's a good idea."

"It's an excellent idea," he insisted. "Knowing the strengths and weaknesses of our competition is the best way to build a strategy for success."

"Yes. But…"

"But?"

She lifted her gaze to find his brow arched in amusement, and felt her cheeks heat anew. "But we agreed to minimize the time we spend together. Remember?"

His mouth crooked in a smile that managed to both scold and tease. "Are you telling me you can't separate your role as my head pastry chef from your former role in my bed while we conduct a bit of hotel business?"

Chastened, she felt her blush burn even hotter. "No."

"Then it's settled. We'll start with Antoine's just as soon as we're finished here."

A knock against the door kept her from protesting further.

They turned to find Stephen's secretary at the door, holding it wide while a stunning brunette in a maroon suit and four-inch heels minced her way into the room.

"Sorry I'm late," she said, her eyes sweeping over Stephen with a hungry gleam. Petite to the point of being delicate, the woman carried a large box filled with fabric swatches, paint wheels, wallpaper samples, and curling carpet squares. "You know how traffic is."

"Of course." Stephen strode forward to relieve the gorgeous designer of her unwieldy burden, and offered her a smile that made Colette's heart twist.

"Thank you," the woman gushed, moving to squeeze Stephen's bulging biceps. "You're always such a gentleman, Mr. Whitfield."

"Ms. Turner, I'd like you to meet Ms. Huntington, one of Doux Rêves's managers."

Jealousy she had no right to feel roared within Colette's chest, but she donned a welcoming smile and moved to offer her hand. "Nice to meet you," she said. "And, please, call me Colette."

"Genevieve," the woman intoned, flicking her gaze over Colette's body and then dismissing her without so much as a smile. "I understand you want to update the bakery and pastry shop here?" she said to Stephen. "Have you a vision for what you want?"

"Yes," he said. Colette turned to find Stephen's eyes fixed on hers. "And Colette here will be your main contact for the job."

Genevieve's gorgeous mouth pursed with a pout. "But I thought—"

"Why don't you two set up a few times to meet this week while I go fetch my car?" He offered a farewell smile to the disgruntled designer, pulled back his sleeve to reveal a thin platinum watch that undoubtedly cost more than she'd earned in the last six months, and then returned his gaze to Colette. "Will five minutes suffice, or do you need more time?"

I need more time.

Used to be one sultry look from Stephen and Colette would cancel her plans, push any appointments she'd scheduled, and drop everything to be with him. Nothing had mattered more than time with Stephen. He'd trumped it all.

But not now. Not anymore. Now she only agreed to be with him under duress. Under the guise of business. She'd do the job she'd been paid to do, and when she was done she'd go home to Emma and her real life. She'd go home to a world that had no place in it for the one man she couldn't afford to want.

"Colette?" he said, reminding her that he awaited her response.

"What? Oh. Right," she blurted. "Five minutes. I'll meet you downstairs as soon as we've compared calendars."

"Excellent. I'll be at the front."

Colette turned back to find Genevieve glaring daggers at her. "Don't delude yourself into thinking you have a chance with him."

As if she needed the reminder.

CHAPTER FIVE

STEPHEN congratulated himself on his stroke of genius the moment he saw Colette exit the elegant entrance to the Renaissance and stride toward him. The bright sunlight caught in her hair and kissed her glowing skin, making her look like a harvest goddess brought to life. She wore her hair up again, exposing the long line of her neck and making his fingers itch to unpin all those tawny curls. Tall, beautiful and vibrant, she looked better than every memory he'd ever had of her. And he had her all to himself for the afternoon.

"Did you find some times to meet with Genevieve?" he asked as he opened her door and gestured her forward.

"Yes," she said in a guarded voice. Her gaze flicked from the interior of his silver Maserati to his braced arm and she stood immobile for a moment, hesitating as if she stood on the edge of a perilous cliff.

"Relax," he told her, moving his free hand to graze the base of her spine. "I'm a safe driver."

She lurched away from his touch and dropped into the cream leather seat without further urging, then reached to buckle her seatbelt. A hint of bare leg flashed before she tucked her skirt over her bent knees. Her spine was so tense it barely touched the back of his low seat.

Watching as she tried to hide from him, he felt a sudden

urge roar through him to drag up her prim skirt and chart the constellation of new freckles he'd glimpsed.

He held himself in check, his muscles tightening to stone. He was not an unprincipled beast. He could control his baser instincts.

So Stephen closed her door with a soft click and dragged in a steadying breath, forcing his desire for Colette into submission. God, he wanted her. Despite everything, he still wanted her. He wanted her smooth skin, her mouth beneath his, her soft cries of completion. He wanted to watch her throat work while he pleasured her, to seat himself so deep between her thighs that neither of them knew where one ended and the other began.

He rounded the car and then slid into his own seat. The interior smelled faintly of her, of vanilla and a warm, spicy note of some tropical flower. Putting the car into gear, his big hand close to her bent legs, he eased out a breath as he inched his way out into the New York traffic. They drove in silence, he checking his GPS and she clutching her purse, until they arrived at the hotel housing Antoine's, the small, intimate French patisserie. After leaving his car with the valet and escorting her to the boutique café, he directed her to a corner table for two that offered an unobstructed view of the display case.

"So, Colette," he said, after ordering a sampler plate and espressos for them both. "You still haven't told me why you left London."

The fork she'd been fingering clattered to the table while a delicate flush painted her cheeks. Pressing her lips together and avoiding his eyes, she surveyed the small cafe and its clustered clientele. "The seating is a bit cramped, don't you think?" she finally asked. "It feels like we're sharing a table with twenty people instead of just two."

He remained silent, waiting to see what other diversionary tactic she tried.

She collected her napkin from the table and smoothed it over her knees before bending to look at the menu. "But the menu's excellent. It offers a good variety of choices and has a wonderful layout."

"Impressive." He allowed himself a small smile.

She cast him a questioning look without straightening from her perusal of the menu.

"I wouldn't have thought it possible to be better at avoidance than you were five years ago."

She inhaled sharply and then dropped her focus back to the menu. "I thought you wanted my opinion on the competition."

"I do." He leaned back in his chair, studying the off-center part of her tipped head. It was as if all the work he'd done breaking down her barriers five years ago didn't matter. He had to start all over. Again. And the hell of it was, he had no idea why. Something had changed. Something big. Something that filled her eyes with nervous apprehension and made her act like a skittish mouse to his hawk. "Among other things," he added.

She stiffened while fresh color seeped into her cheeks. "This is supposed to be a professional outing. Remember?"

"Yes," he said as his gaze traced the line of her brow, her cheek, the narrow bridge of her freckled nose. "But I believe in multitasking. Surely you recall that about me?"

"And you wonder why I was reluctant to accompany you," she muttered.

Amused, intrigued, and more interested in her explanation than he probably should be, he leaned forward and splayed his hands atop the middle of their small table. He remembered their last night together in her bed, the only time she'd allowed him in her small, intimate apartment. After finally gaining her trust enough for her to let him in, he'd felt like celebrating his triumph. He'd finally cleared the last hurdle of her defenses. He'd gone to sleep with a smile on his face, both of them spent and their damp limbs tangled in her twisted sheets.

Then something had spooked her. Something that had sent her scurrying away like a thief in the night.

"Are your reasons really so confidential that you still can't tell me after all this time?" he asked.

She fidgeted beneath his stare, pleating and unpleating the linen napkin in her lap. "Why would you even care?"

"Call it a loose end."

"A loose end?" A scowl flitted over her features and then just as quickly disappeared, piquing his curiosity even more.

"Would you prefer I call it something else?"

She pursed her lips in obvious frustration, and then lifted her defiant gaze to his. "The only reason you want to know is because I left you instead of the other way around. Had I waited until you returned from Paris, and given you another few weeks to break things off yourself, we wouldn't even be having this conversation."

"I had no plans to break things off with you, Colette," he corrected her. "You just assumed I did."

"With good reason, given your past history," she insisted.

"You were nothing like the lovers of my past."

"Even so, you had no interest in anything beyond what we had."

"I seem to remember you sharing that interest."

"You're right," she admitted, though it didn't sound like she believed her own assertion. "So why the inquisition, when we promised no questions?"

He lifted on shoulder in a deliberately casual shrug. "I'm curious."

"No. You accuse me of wanting control, but you're just as

bad. Something doesn't end the way you want it to, and you can't leave it alone."

"Humor me."

"Fine," she said on a sharp exhale. "You want to know why I left? I left because I was no longer interested in a go-nowhere relationship." Her voice dared him to deny her claim, to rewrite the history he'd replayed again and again. "I was bumping up against your internal relationship deadline, and I saw no need to postpone the inevitable."

It stung more than he cared to admit, hearing how she thought of him and remembering the way she'd discarded him without a moment's hesitation. Yes, they'd set up their relationship that way initially, but he'd been open to renegotiation. "I don't have an internal relationship deadline," he countered, and he heard the defensive note in his voice.

"No?" She laughed, and it was a brittle, dismissive sound. "Then tell me the name of even one woman who's maintained your interest for longer than six months."

He might have bought her edge of cynicism, might even have reacted to the note of accusation in her tone, had he not seen the infinitesimal flash of pain in her hazel eyes. But he did. He saw it. *Felt* it. And he grappled with the crazy impulse to haul her into his arms and promise never to hurt her again. Which made no sense, because he wasn't the one who'd hurt her. *She'd* been the one to leave, the one to give up on them before he had a chance to convince her otherwise. "You left because you thought I'd get bored?"

"Of course! It was only a matter of time before you tired of me," she said. "I had a month. Two, tops. Before someone new caught your interest."

He stared at her for a long, silent moment before asking, "What makes you so sure?"

"You made me sure. Remember? You never once indicated

that you wanted anything long-term, and I didn't see the point
of waiting around for the other shoe to drop."

"Colette—"

"No. You're a Whitfield and I'm just a nobody who worked
in your kitchen."

"I never thought of you as a nobody."

"But it's the truth nonetheless." She blew out a sigh, looking oddly deflated. "Look. I'll never deny that I had a wonderful time for the five months I spent with you. But it wasn't
a real relationship." Her mouth curved into a sad crescent
filled with regret and apology. "What kind of fool would I
have been to behave as if it were?"

Hearing her bald delivery of the truth rankled, unearth-
ing an uncomfortable blend of irritation and irrational guilt.
She was right. They'd never claimed to want more than the
pleasure they brought each other's bodies. That was one of
the reasons he'd liked her so much. Her willingness to expect no more than he could give, her total lack of pressure,
had been liberating. Exhilarating. "Are you telling me you
wanted more, but were too afraid to ask?" he queried.

Her features softened into something horrifically close to
pity. "No, Stephen. I'm telling you that we were over."

He cleared his throat and pulled his hands from the table,
remembering the surge of excitement that had gripped his
chest once he'd realized he'd stumbled upon Colette again.
Embarrassing, really, how quickly she'd burrowed beneath
his skin, how quickly he'd fallen back under her spell. "So
that was it?" he clarified. "You wanted to spare yourself the
pain of my rejection, and decided to take matters into your
hands? To end things on *your* timetable so I wouldn't have
to."

"Yes."

"Well, thank you for telling me," he said in a flat voice.
"For clearing up the mystery at last."

She studied his carefully blank expression, her brows notched in confusion. "I'd think you'd be grateful I didn't cling to you, wailing out my heartbreak and begging you to stay," she said, as if trying to soothe his stinging pride. "Unlike all your previous lovers, I spared you the discomfort of a messy, emotional scene."

"You're right." He forced a smile as their sampler plate arrived, an array of bite-size morsels of lemon cake, coconut tuiles and hazelnut cookies he no longer had any interest in consuming. He lifted his espresso cup and tipped it toward her in a silent toast. "You did us both a favor, leaving me without a backward glance."

Her face paled just a bit in the early afternoon light, her freckles suddenly more pronounced than they'd been before. "Yes," she agreed with a slight dip of her head. "I did."

Report to my office. Now. Two days later, Stephen's delivered message sent worry spiking through Colette's chest. She didn't want to report to his office. She didn't want to report to Stephen ever again.

It was too hard feigning indifference when he made all her senses come alive.

Knowing he could still turn her emotions inside out, she took several deep breaths, ordered her heart to beat normally and her body to remain calm.

He was waiting for her when the elevator doors slid open, looking far too authoritative, controlled and male for her comfort. Watching his black pupils flare as his gaze skimmed her body, she wished she'd worn something less form-fitting than her brown Capri pants and a coral sleeveless sweater. It was easier to negotiate when she wasn't so aware of him as a man. Or when she wasn't so aware of herself as a woman.

"You're late," he said.

"I just got your message two minutes ago."

He ushered her past his secretary and into his office, gesturing her toward his desk and the comfortable chair placed before it. She stopped at its polished mahogany edge, not willing to sit down.

"I met with Genevieve this morning," he said, his expression inscrutable.

Inhaling past her irritation, Colette braced her shoulders and said, "I figured as much." She'd expected him to be impatient with the lack of progress they'd made. The woman's hourly rate couldn't be cheap, and so far they'd found little to agree upon in the pastry shop's design plan. "She was quite upset when she left."

"It seems you've been quite inflexible regarding how the Doux Rêves should look and feel."

She angled her chin up. "If you don't want my input, I'm happy to step aside."

"Are you?" he murmured, his eyes fastened on hers.

Annoyance simmered within Colette's chest, but she kept her voice calm. She knew Genevieve had complained to Stephen, and, given Colette's lack of experience and training in interior design, she was fully prepared to have her ideas shot down. But defending herself simply because she had a different opinion was not what she'd agreed to. "Yes. You can let Henri deal with her and I'll just return to my baking."

"That's your solution?" he asked with an amused smile. "Sic Henri on her?"

Colette pressed her mouth into a grim line. "Why not? If Genevieve thinks *I'm* inflexible, she's in for a surprise."

"I don't doubt that." A slow smile gathered behind his eyes, warming the blue and making her stomach flip in response. "But I don't think it's necessary to take such extreme measures."

She glared at him. "Don't patronize me."

"I'm not. I fired Genevieve half an hour ago."

Rendered speechless by the pronouncement, she could only gape at him as he moved close enough to curve his large hand around her bare upper arm.

"I trust you, Colette, and I value your opinion." He squeezed her arm, imparting his support and his willingness to stand by her decisions. "I suspect she knew that, and felt threatened by you."

Her arm tingled beneath his touch, sending rivulets of awareness down to her stomach and legs. "That's ridiculous," she said, striving for a calm, unaffected tone.

"Is it?" His lifted brow belied her words. "I'm sure it took her all of one second to figure out that there's something between us."

"There's nothing between us." *There can't be.*

He ignored her as if she hadn't spoken and his thumb idly brushed the skin along her arm, perilously close to the swell of her breast. "I can't work with people who allow their personal insecurities to interfere with what's best for my business."

She swallowed, exquisitely aware of that steady back and forth sweep of his thumb. "You slept with her, didn't you?"

Amusement flickered in his eyes. "Why do you always assume the worst of me?"

Her cell phone buzzed within her back pocket, making her jump. Since Janet and Henri were the only people who knew her number, and neither of them would call in the middle of the day unless it were important, she winced and reached for the phone. "Do you mind?"

The phone buzzed again, and Stephen arched a brow as his hand fell to his side. "Do I mind that you're accepting personal calls during a business meeting with me?"

She held up a finger while her eyes flicked to the phone's screen. Janet. Without thinking about the consequences, she accepted the call, turned her back, and pressed the phone to her ear. "What is it?" she asked. "Is everything okay?"

Janet's tinkle of laughter sounded in her ear. "Of course it is! Everything's fine, dear. I just wanted to let you know we're going to the park for a bit of playtime and I didn't want you to get worried if you called and we were out."

Janet refused to carry a cell phone, stating that she had no head for any of those newfangled gadgets. Closing her eyes, Colette decided she was going to make it a condition of her employment from here on out. She cupped her hand over her mouth, straining for privacy though there was none to be had. "Thank you," she said in a low voice, cursing Janet's poor timing but unable to fault her for the call. "I appreciate it."

"You're welcome."

"Don't forget sunblock," she added in a whisper.

"You're talking too softly, dear. I can't hear you."

Colette bit back a frustrated groan. "Sunblock," she repeated a little louder. "Don't forget."

"Ah, of course. And I'll have Emma wear her cute little hat, too."

"Thank you."

When she returned the phone to her pocket, she felt Stephen's regard against the back of her head.

"Sunblock?" he observed dryly. "Who calls to discuss sunblock in the middle of the workday?"

Her thoughts ricocheted from one prospective lie to another, even as she summoned a bland smile and a composure she didn't feel. "It was my roommate," she said as she turned back to face him. "She has very sensitive skin and burns quite easily."

Surprise lifted his brow. "You have a roommate?"

"Yes."

"Who checks in with you while you're working?"

She felt herself flush. "Don't tell me you're interested in a routine conversation between my roommate and me?"

"Haven't you figured it out yet?" His lids lowered as his gaze dipped to her mouth. "I'm interested in everything about you."

The flush burned hotter and she fought the urge to lick her suddenly dry lips. "You and I were talking about Genevieve and the fact that you fired her." She walked to his office doorway and turned. "If there's nothing else, then I assume our meeting is concluded?"

"You assume wrong."

"You've hired her replacement already?"

"Yes," Stephen said, moving to tower over her where she stood. "I thought we'd go with a male this time. So there's no competition for my attention and approval."

She did lick her lips this time, her pulse kicking with denial. "There was no competition with Genevieve."

His eyes warmed. "You've got that right."

She firmed her mouth. She would not allow him to see that his nearness disconcerted her. "There was no competition because I was not competing."

"Our new designer can't start until tomorrow, which means you have the rest of the day free." He grinned, cocking his head as his gaze trailed over her face. "Care to continue this conversation over lunch?"

"No," she told him as she stepped out into the hall and walked toward the elevator. "There's nothing else to discuss until the designer arrives."

"I can think of plenty to discuss," Stephen said as he caught up to her and waylaid her departure with a hand upon her elbow. He loved that she'd chosen a sleeveless top today; he loved the access it provided to her soft, soft skin. "This new roommate of yours, for instance. How did you two meet?"

Her face blanched and she yanked her arm away to press

the elevator button. "I don't see that it's any business of yours."

He stood beside her, trying to read the thoughts churning behind those averted hazel eyes and remembering her furtive phone conversation with her roommate. She'd acted like he'd caught her stealing towels from the hotel laundry room, her evasive responses to his questions not quite ringing true.

"What are you hiding?"

"Nothing."

He frowned. What if this roommate of hers was a boyfriend? A boyfriend she'd claimed not to have?

His hands tightened at the thought. Though it would hardly be fair to expect her to remain perennially single, he found that the prospect of her having another lover didn't sit well in his gut. In fact, it made him want to hit something. Hard.

The familiar ding signaled the elevator's arrival and she scurried inside without answering his question.

"Who is this roommate of yours, exactly?" he persisted.

"It doesn't concern you," she said.

"When his calls interrupt my meetings, it does."

"It won't happen again," she told the sliding doors.

"Still doesn't make up for today. We lost time."

She turned to face him, her rising temper making her golden eyes flash. "Five seconds, maybe! It's hardly worth mentioning!"

"My time is very valuable," he said with a bland stare. "I'm afraid you'll just have to make it up to me."

"Right." She scowled, the fire in her eyes sending an arrow of heat to his groin. "You'll demand an extra three hours of my time since mine is worth so much less than yours, right?"

"You make me sound so unreasonable," he said, in a deliberately reasonable tone.

"Only because you are," she snapped.

"Have lunch with me, and I'll call it even."

Her expression flattened into mulishness. "No."

"We both have to eat. Why not kill two birds with one stone?"

"Because I don't want to eat lunch with you," she huffed. "If I'm not needed here, I'd rather go home."

He smiled. "I don't have a problem eating lunch at your house."

"No!"

"No?" He shrugged one shoulder, wondering why she looked so distressed. "I could meet your roommate. See your house."

Her eyes flared in alarm. "Absolutely not."

"Then let me grab something for us from across the street. We'll eat in the courtyard, just two business colleagues sharing a meal."

"I—"

"We're here," he interrupted. "Go save us a spot. I'll meet you in ten minutes."

CHAPTER SIX

TEN minutes later, Stephen scanned the busy courtyard for a second time, the bagged lunches growing tepid and soggy in the afternoon heat. Colette, true to form, had not done as she'd been told.

The stubborn minx.

Fortunately, he could prove just as stubborn as she. So he spun on his heel and headed toward HR, intent on finding her address and tracking her down regardless. He wanted to meet this *roommate* of hers, anyway.

By the time he found her house, a cozy little cottage nearly twenty minutes outside Manhattan, his curiosity had been more than piqued. To keep his arrival off her radar, he'd driven a less flashy car, a small black BMW that blended in with the other vehicles of the city. He was grateful for his anonymity now, seeing the house she'd chosen. The tidy, whitewashed home looked like it had been built fifty years ago, with neat yellow shutters and window boxes overflowing with pink and purple flowers. His brow furrowed in confusion.

Colette had always claimed to prefer low-maintenance flats, the smaller the better. He'd never known a female to care less about material things, and she'd had no interest in shopping for home décor. Aside from her kitchen, she'd spent no money on feminine fripperies or coordinated furniture. She'd told him she was all about functionality and efficiency, and his one foray into her personal space had proved her claim.

Looking at the modest little house, surrounded by a well-groomed lawn, tidily trimmed bushes, and a pocket-size flower garden, he felt an unexpected spike of jealousy stab at his chest. Colette, who'd only allowed him in her flat one time, had set up a proper home with a roommate. A roommate who called her in the middle of the day to talk about nonsensical things. A roommate she didn't want Stephen to meet.

Unwilling to mull over the possibilities any longer without knowing the truth, he shoved open his door, exited his car, and strode across the narrow paved street. The punishing slap of his heels against the blacktop matched his mood exactly. He'd be damned if he'd allow her to keep lying to him. After all the time they'd spent together, she owed him the truth.

He'd already framed his opening sentence when he stabbed his thumb into the doorbell.

The doorbell echoed somewhere in the back of the house, followed by a high-pitched squeal and a low, feminine murmur.

The front door opened to reveal a miniature version of Colette, dressed in a cloud of ruffled pink, her tousled yellow curls forming a bright halo of gold about her small upturned face.

"Hi!" she said with a grin, just as a plump gray-haired woman in a flowered housedress joined her at the door.

"Emma!" she said in exasperation. "How many times have I told you not to open the door to strangers?"

The child's eyes widened and she gasped aloud before slamming the door shut between them.

For a protracted beat of time, Stephen simply stared at the closed door in shock. *Colette was a mother?*

The door opened again, this time to reveal the older woman and child standing side by side.

"Sorry," the woman began. "We—"

"You're a stranger," the girl announced, cocking her head in a perfect imitation of her mother. "'Cause I don't know you yet."

Stephen blinked, trying to adjust to his sense of vertigo while taking in the child's small rosebud mouth, obstinate chin, and large, wide-set eyes the color of a summer sky. "Yes, I guess I am." Recovering his manners, he bent to address the child. "My name's Stephen. What's yours?"

Rather than answering, the child turned her inquisitive face toward the older woman and whispered, "Can I tell him?"

"As I was saying," the woman said, her face creasing in a smile, "we're still working on how we interact with strangers." She returned her focus to the little girl and nodded. "Yes, you may tell him your name."

"I'm Emma Huntington." She gripped the woman's skirt in one small white hand and hopped to a sneakered foot. "An' I like jumping."

"I can see that," he said, slowly straightening as the child's full name sank in. Apparently this enchanting child belonged to Colette and Colette alone. Where was the father? Had he abandoned them both? Or was he her *roommate*? Suddenly, the thought of her bearing another man's child, sharing his bed and opening her heart when it had always remained closed to him, had jealousy pinching his chest. But he forced a bland calmness to his voice and lifted his attention to the older woman. "Is Colette home?"

"Not at the moment," said the older woman, her brows lowering as she scanned his face. "May I deliver a message?"

Aware that he didn't wish to arouse her suspicions, Stephen schooled his features into the smile guaranteed to make any woman soften. "When do you expect her back?"

"Momma's working at the hotel," volunteered Emma as she switched to hop on the other foot, stabilizing her balance with a twisted grip in the older woman's skirt. "She makes desserts."

Stephen's lungs tightened as he looked down at Colette's daughter. He didn't like that Colette had moved on without him, that she'd made a life, created a child, and cut him so completely out of her future. She'd never looked back, even once, and the proof of her decision stared up at him with bright blue eyes. "Yes, I know," he agreed. "Your mother is a very good chef."

"She's gonna teach me to make cookies!"

"Then you are a lucky girl. Just like I'm lucky to have her as an employee."

Emma's face screwed up in confusion and her hopping stalled. "What's a employee?"

"*You're* Colette's new boss?" the older woman gasped. "The one from England?"

"Yes," he said, lifting his head and smiling in acknowledgment. "I'm Stephen Whitfield. Did Colette mention me?"

"Of course she did!" she scolded as she swung the door wide. "And if I'd known who you were, I'd have invited you in right away!"

What did she tell you? "Thank you," he said as he stepped over the threshold.

"Colette called about a half hour ago," she said as she and the child moved to make room in the narrow hallway. "She should be home any minute."

"Excellent," he said, flashing a smile that felt uncomfortable and strained. "I was hoping I'd catch her."

"Momma likes to tuck me in for my nap," offered Emma.

The nanny reached to collect the child's small hand and ushered her down the hall before turning right into another room. "Can I fetch you some iced tea while you wait?" she called over her shoulder.

"Thank you, Mrs....?" he said, as he followed the duo into a small, cheerful room littered with toys.

"Smith," she said, releasing her young charge and then turning to face Stephen with a wide, flattered smile. "Though you can call me Janet."

Stephen nodded while Emma bounded toward a toy box in the corner. Within seconds she'd retrieved a half-dressed doll with pink marker all over its face. "This is Chrissie," she said, returning to his side and holding the doll out for his inspection. "I accidentally drawed on her face, but she didn't get mad."

"Emma, why don't you come help me fetch Mr. Whitfield's tea?"

"But I wanna show him—!"

"It's all right," Stephen interrupted, moving to lower himself into a chair upholstered in striped fabric and then beckoning toward the child. "Emma can keep me company while I wait."

Mrs. Smith hesitated while Emma rushed forward to shove Chrissie into his big hands. "She's got blond hair, just like me. An' she likes pink, too."

"Does she, now?" he said, lifting the doll and setting it atop his knee.

"I don't know about this, Mr. Whitfield," said Janet as she hovered near the doorway looking worried. "Have you much experience with children? Emma can be quite a talkative handful."

"Please. Call me Stephen," he said easily. "And, yes. Between all my maternal cousins I've had practice with dozens of children of assorted shapes and sizes. Emma and I will get along just fine while we wait."

"Oh. I suppose it'll be all right, then," she said, pointing a finger toward Emma. "You be a good girl, you hear? Don't ask too many questions and mind your manners."

"I will!" the child assured her with a sunny smile.

"I'll be back in a tick," the woman said, bustling off to the kitchen.

Before Janet disappeared from view, Emma had already shifted her attention back to Stephen. "You talk funny."

"That's because I live in England."

"Momma lived in England," the child said, her expression a skeptical combination of accusation and scold. "But she doesn't talk funny."

"You're right," he admitted with a smile, realizing that the child was just as wary of liars as her mother was. "She doesn't. But she didn't live there as long as I have."

The explanation seemed to satisfy her, because Emma moved closer to adjust her doll into a sleeping position on his lap. "Chrissie's tired," she said. "She needs lots of naps 'cause she's just a baby."

"I can tell," he agreed amiably as he eyed the bedraggled Chrissie, with her vandalized plastic skin and closed eyes. "She must spend a lot of time sleeping."

"I only have to take one nap," she confided, leaning close against his knee. "'Cause I'm a big girl."

"Are you, now?"

She grinned, exposing a row of tiny white teeth as she held up four dimpled fingers. "Yes. I'm four-'n-a-half."

"Four and a half!" He gasped in feigned shock, while mentally tacking on nine months and coming up long. Colette certainly hadn't wasted any time finding another man. "How did you get to be so old?"

"I have birthdays, silly!"

"You do?" He cocked his head and studied the small child, wondering exactly how old she was. "Do you know when your birthday is?"

"'Course I do!" She abandoned his knee and rushed to forage for yet another prize to show him, this one a pink ruffled strip of fabric with some sort of sparkly tiara attached to it. "Santa brought this for my birthday."

"He did?"

"Uh-huh." She pushed the crown on over her curls and

arranged the pink train over her shoulder before coming back to show him the multiple tiers of lace and ribbon. "Momma says I get extra-special presents 'cause I'm her extra-special Christmas gift."

He stopped breathing as he did the mental math, his thoughts reeling with the implications of Emma's birth date. Emma had been born on Christmas. *Christmas.* Which meant either Colette had cheated on him, made a child with another man at the same time they'd been together, or *he* was a father.

But that was impossible. They'd used protection.

Every time.

"I'm a princess, see?" Emma pointed out, dragging his attention back to the here and now.

"What?" He stared at the child as she curtsied before him, his sense of vertigo rushing back tenfold as belated recognition slammed hard into his gut.

Emma didn't look up at him with the curious hazel eyes of her mother.

No. She looked at him with the bright, distinctive blue eyes every single Whitfield for countless generations had shared. The eyes she'd inherited from her father. From *him.*

"You look funny," she said, leaning forward to tug on his hand.

His breath escaped in a ragged rush.

"Does your tummy hurt?" she asked, screwing up her tiny nose.

He blinked and drew in a steadying breath, forcing a smile to his face. "No, sweetheart," he said. "I'm just thinking about your mother and how happy she must be to have you."

"Momma loves me a lot," Emma agreed. "She says I'm her angel. But I don't want to be an angel. I want to be a princess."

Suddenly everything clicked into place: Colette's reason for leaving, her continued secrecy, her *roommate.* She'd borne him a daughter and she'd never breathed a word of it to him.

"Do you like princesses?"

He looked down at his beautiful daughter, the daughter he hadn't even known existed, and anger at missing her birth, her first breath, first tooth, first *everything* twisted low in his gut. How could Colette have stolen four years from him? Four and a half *years*!

"I adore princesses," he said in a soft voice. "Especially pretty princesses with blond hair and blue eyes."

Now that he knew to look for it, he could trace the stamp of the Whitfield genes even more readily than before. He saw the trademark cowlick on the right side of her forehead that he and grandfather shared. He saw his own straight brows and the same bow in her upper lip.

"You do?" Emma's face—his *daughter's* face!—lit up with her smile and an unexpected tightness took hold of his chest. *Damn* Colette. She had some serious explaining to do, and this time she wasn't escaping without telling him the truth.

The front screen door squeaked open and he heard Colette step into the home she'd chosen for their child. "Janet?" she called. "You haven't put Emma down for her nap yet, have you?"

Stephen watched as Colette rounded the corner into the living room. Stumbling in shocked recognition, she froze and the blood drained from her face.

"Welcome home, Colette," he said grimly, surprised that he sounded so calm when he felt like wringing her beautiful, duplicitous neck. "Or should I say *Mummy?*"

"Stephen," she started, her lips trembling within her white face. "What are you doing here?"

He surged to his feet, the urge to shake her tearing through him with seismic fury. "I don't think you're in any position to ask questions," he said, in an ominously quiet voice.

"I—"

"How is it that you have a four-year-old daughter I knew nothing about?"

Her hazel eyes darted frantically toward Emma and then back again. Fear was stamped in every fierce line of her face. "Not here, Stephen. Please not here—"

"Mr. Whitfield held Chrissie while she taked her nap," interrupted Emma. "An' he likes princesses, too. He said so."

"That's right, Emma," he said, in a low, conversational voice. "Little blue-eyed princesses are a personal favorite of mine."

"Don't…" Colette began again, her arms wrapping about her ribs while a glimmer of tears gathered in her distressed eyes. "She doesn't…"

"Why didn't you tell me?"

"B-because," she stammered, her gaze ricocheting from Emma's curious face to his and back again. "I…"

"You?"

"I wanted to keep her safe."

A rage he hadn't felt for twenty-five long, long years made his chest burn hot and laced his words with a dangerous, deadly calm. "I suggest you tell Janet she's on duty for a little while longer," he said grimly. "You and I have some serious items to discuss."

She flinched, and then swiftly recovered, her chin lifting while her slim shoulders braced for the worst. Her flashing hazel gaze, limned with a disconcerting blend of righteous indignation and fear, collided with his and held. "Fine, we'll talk. *In private*," she said, smiling down at Emma as if she needed to protect her. "Emma, sweetheart, why don't you go find Janet while Mr. Whitfield and I have a grownup talk outside?"

CHAPTER SEVEN

"START talking," he said, the moment they were alone in her tiny yard.

"Not here," Colette replied, striding across the street while she frantically tried to collect her thoughts. "I don't want Janet or Emma to hear us fighting."

"Oh, we're not going to fight," he said, in a deceptively mild voice that sent a tremor of unease down her spine. "This is no lovers' squabble." He gripped her upper arm and escorted her to his car, then loomed over her, his brittle blue eyes daring her to refute him. "This is you telling me exactly what I want to hear, followed by you listening as I tell you how we're going to handle it."

"But—"

"No." He cut her off with a harrowing slice of his hand. "This is my child we're talking about, and you've lost the right to offer input."

"But I'm her mother!" she protested. "I've only done what I thought was best."

"What *you* thought? What about what *I* thought?"

"You were never part of the decision."

"Exactly," he growled. "You thought it was *best* to keep her from knowing her father," he said, leaning forward to bracket her within the cage of his powerful arms. "You thought it was *best* to hide her from the man who gave her life, the man who could give her everything."

"Except what she needed most!" she blurted, her frantic pulse clubbing hard against her chest. "You'd only hurt her, and I couldn't allow that!"

Ice slammed into his eyes, and his voice assumed a frigid edge. "*Hurt* her? You think I'd hurt my own daughter? Good God, Colette, what kind of monster do you think I am?"

"The kind that doesn't know the first thing about commitment. The kind who has no desire to settle down or give up his playboy lifestyle to raise a child!"

"Since when does my desire to not settle down translate into an inability to do the right thing by my child?"

"Are you serious?" She stared at him, wondering how he could even ask. "You're only interested in temporary flings, and fatherhood is a permanent gig."

"Who the hell gave you the right to determine what my interests are?" he snapped.

She firmed her jaw, knowing she was right. "You did. You said you didn't want children. On multiple occasions. You said you'd never bring another Whitfield into the world."

"Only because I didn't want to subject a child to the life I'd had," he ground out. "I certainly didn't mean I couldn't accept my responsibilities when our protection failed us."

"And there's the difference. I don't view Emma as a failure or an accident or a plan gone awry. She's a child. A precious, beautiful child who deserves to be wanted. And I won't ever allow my daughter to feel otherwise."

"*Your* daughter?"

She straightened her spine, pressing against his car and putting as much distance between them as possible. "I'm the only one who wants her."

"You're wrong."

"No, I'm not. You just think you want her right now. Once you've had a few moments to adjust to the shock, you'll realize I made the right choice for everybody. A child has needs,

Stephen, needs that don't vanish simply because you tire of meeting them."

"I'm aware of that." Palpable anger knotted his jaw as he bowed over her. "And I'm perfectly capable of committing to my child and providing her with everything she needs."

"Are you really?" she pressed. "Because last I heard you were incapable of feeling that tense, messy emotion called love."

His nostrils flared as he glared at her. "Love doesn't feed or clothe a child."

"No," she agreed, hiking her chin. "But it makes her feel happy and safe and wanted. Emotions you'll strip from her if you make her feel like an accident that wasn't supposed to happen."

"I would never make her feel that way."

"You say that now."

"So, what? You're calling me a liar now?" He laughed, and it was a biting, humorless sound. "Oh, that's rich."

"I didn't lie. I just omitted the truth," she blurted. "And you can't blame me for it. We both know what would have happened if I'd told you I was pregnant with your child."

"No, we don't know. Because you made sure nothing could happen," he bit out. "You gave me no chance to react at all."

"Because I already knew how you'd react."

"How could you possibly know, when I don't even know myself?" he asked, frustrated anger sharpening his tone to a razor-thin edge.

"Tell me, then. Tell me what you would have done had I told you. No. Wait," she scoffed, holding her hand aloft. "I already know. You'd have shouldered the mantle of responsibility like all decent men do. You'd have pushed aside your reservations and your resentment and done the *right* thing. You'd have forced me to marry you, felt trapped against your will, and then taken out your frustration on both me and my daughter for the rest of your life."

"You don't know that."

"I do. Parenthood, especially when you're in it out of obligation, isn't all fun and games. When the newness of having a child wears off, the reality and the permanence of it sets in. I know it, you know it, and I won't have my daughter go through the pain of your resentment just because a playboy happened to get one of his flings pregnant."

"What makes you so sure I'd resent it?" he flung back, leaning close enough that she could see the hot flare of rage in his eyes. "When *you're* the one who couldn't handle the intimacy of a real relationship?"

"You want to blame it on me? Fine," she said, the old pain twisting deep in her bones. "I can handle your hatred. Emma can't."

He looked at her in grim silence, the muscles of his forearms flexing as he debated his next words.

Try and deny it, she thought. *Try and claim you're capable of loving a child you never wanted to have.*

"I would never hate my own child," he finally said. "You're wrong to assume I would."

"I'm not," she said, swallowing hard against the knot crowding her throat. "Men with your past do not do well with fatherhood. There are thousands of unwanted children out there who can attest to the fact."

"I am not one of those men."

"Well, I can't take that risk. And neither can Emma."

"Too bad. It's no longer your choice."

His words sent a chill through her veins. "What are you saying?" she breathed.

"You know exactly what I'm saying, Colette," he said, the flinty anger in his eyes promising the retribution she'd feared since the day she'd watched that first pregnancy test strip turn blue. "Because I *am* going to do the right thing, five years too late. We're getting married. Tomorrow."

"No."

"Yes. You marry me or I take you to court to establish my parental rights. I use my wealth and my connections to wage a legal war for custody you're incapable of winning."

"You wouldn't dare!" she breathed.

"Try me," he said with an implacable stare.

"But I can't marry you!" she gasped. "You're insane to think I'd agree to that!"

He glared at her. "You're insane to think I'll settle for anything less."

Her pulse rioted beneath the surface of her skin while her mind raced with alternatives. She could skip town again. She could hide. Change her name, move to a small Midwestern American town, and live off cash earned waiting tables. He'd never find her.

"And don't even think about running away again," he warned, reading her thoughts as if she'd spoken them aloud. "Now that I know about Emma, you won't be able to pack so much as a toothbrush without me finding out about it."

"You'd have me followed?"

"Every minute of every day," he continued, his voice filled with a cold, calculated threat that made her legs go numb. "If you even *dream* about stealing Emma from me again, I'll make you pay."

"You can't do that!"

"No? Watch me," he said, as calmly as if he were ordering wine with dinner. "Fight me in this, and I will make your life a living hell."

"Why? Why would you do such a thing?"

"Because I want my daughter, and no one will stop me from having her."

"But you have no interest in fatherhood! Why would you change now?"

"You act like I owe you an explanation. I don't."

"If you try to be her father just because you think it's your duty, because you feel compelled to meet your obligations, you'll only end up hurting her."

"That's a chance you'll have to take, isn't it?" he said, leaning close enough that she could see his pupils flare with banked rage. "Marry me, grant me unlimited access to my child, and you'll be on site to protect her from any harm you think I might cause."

"And what about the rest of the Whitfields? How do I protect her from them?"

"I'll take care of my family."

"How? Your family will never accept me or Emma. You know they won't."

"I don't give a damn about who they will or won't accept. This is *my* life."

"It's not just your life. It's all of our lives now. Yours. Mine. And Emma's. And there's not a single Whitfield who thinks I'm viable wife material. It's unlikely that they'll think any better of our child."

He muttered a quiet oath and then firmed his jaw as he glared at her. "It doesn't matter what they think. Emma is my child, and nothing they say or do changes that fact."

"I heard your grandfather and Liam, Stephen. I heard the things they said about me and my *class*," she insisted.

His jaw flexed while a vein pulsed visibly in his temple. "You weren't supposed to hear that."

"Obviously. But I did. I heard that I didn't belong in your future. I heard that the thought of me having your child would upset everything in your perfect world. So I saved you the hassle of having to deal with us at all."

"That wasn't your choice to make."

"And maybe I'd have made a different one had you given me any reason to reconsider. But instead you told me you were leaving for Paris, claiming we both needed space to think. You abandoned me before you even knew about Emma. It was hardly the opportune time for me to let you know I was pregnant with your child."

"I didn't abandon you. I left because you wanted me to. I've never known a more skittish female, and I was trying to give you what I thought you needed."

"Don't you dare put that on me! You were taking what you needed. You'd just told me you didn't want marriage or the messy emotions of anything more meaningful than a steady bed partner!"

"Did you ever stop to think that maybe I was saying those things because it was what I thought you wanted to hear?"

"Right. Because every woman is just *dying* to hear that she's a good shag and nothing more."

"You're not every woman, damn it!"

"So why do you want to marry me, then?"

"Maybe I want that steady bed partner back again," he said. His mouth tightened while his blue eyes flicked to her mouth, her breasts and then back. "Maybe I'm willing to give up my bachelor status for a consistently good shag."

She sucked in a breath, her body awakening beneath his heated gaze despite his coarse words. "You're a bastard."

"I think that's been established already."

"I won't marry you," she breathed. "Ever."

His arctic gaze glittered with brittle, dangerous threat. "Then don't." His voice lowered to its most ominous range. "Don't marry me, and I'll use every resource I have to take Emma away from you. Permanently."

Panicked, desperate, and blindingly angry, she shoved against his chest with both hands. "Try it, then. Try to take a child away from her mother when your name isn't even on the birth certificate," she challenged. "Try it and see how successful you'll be."

He cocked a brow, obviously unimpressed by both her pitiful attempt to move him and her threat. "No father listed on the birth certificate? You realize, don't you, that omitting the father's name just makes you look worse. Like a woman who's so free with her sexual favors that she doesn't even know who fathered her child."

She felt the blood drain from her face. "No, it doesn't. It makes it look like I didn't want her real father to have any sort of claim on her. That I thought she'd be better off with no father than with a father who'd end up breaking her little heart."

Every muscle in his body went taut while his nostrils pinched white in offense. "I don't care about your motives, and neither will the courts. I'll just get a judge to order a DNA test and then the birth certificate won't matter."

"It will slow you down, though," she said. "Enough for me to lobby a defense you can't overcome. You forget, Stephen. My child loves me. She needs me. And it's in her best welfare to remain with me. There's not a judge anywhere who'd see it differently."

"Oh, I'll find one," he said, sneering down at her mutinous expression. "Money talks, and I'll come after you until you don't have a cent left to wage this little war of yours. And when you run out of everything, when your accounts are stripped to the bone, I'll still come after you. I'll fight for the right to be in my child's life. And I'll win."

"You won't," she insisted.

"Oh? And how will you ensure that when you have no job, no money, and no home to supplement your fight for custody?"

She sucked in a breath, stunned that he'd be so intentionally cruel. "Are you threatening to bankrupt me so fully that it drives your child out her home?" she asked, amazed that she'd once thought herself in love with him.

"I negotiate to win." His icy smile told her he'd yet to lose. "And I always, always win."

She softened her tone and changed tactics, hoping to appeal to his logic. "How is making Emma miserable a win for you? Or for anyone, for that matter?"

"She won't be miserable. I can make my own child happy."

"By taking her away from her mother? By ripping her away from the only parent and home she's ever known?"

"Don't paint me out to be the villain here. *You're* the reason she doesn't know me."

"Yes, but we can't change the past. We can only work with Emma's life now. If you truly wish to be a good father to Emma, you'll care more about her welfare and happiness than your own. Maintaining her sense of security will take precedence over any feud you and I might have."

"Whereas if *you* truly wish to retain your role in Emma's life, you'll accept the inevitable and marry me," he countered. "You'll save Emma the torture of a long, drawn-out fight and just admit defeat."

She shook her head, the sick realization that she might never change his mind settling in her stomach like a stone. "Why would you want to marry me, knowing that I would view it as a defeat?" she asked. Distress made her voice crack. "You can't tell me that's the kind of marriage you want to model for our daughter?"

His expression hardened and she saw the ruthless businessman who always won, the merciless negotiator who went for the jugular, no matter the cost to his personal fortune. "My child deserves my name and an intact family. She deserves to know I am her father."

"Then we'll tell her. Together. And we'll work something out that doesn't make her feel like she's lost her entire world." Colette placed a tentative hand on his forearm, finding it as hard as carved granite. "Please? I swear, we can find a middle ground that doesn't make us all miserable."

A muscle jumped in his jaw. "I have no interest in compromise." He scowled. "Nor in *middle ground*."

"I know you're angry. I know you want to punish me, and I

don't blame you," she said. "But there has to be another way. There has to be a way to fix this without resorting to marriage and compromising our child's happiness."

His nostrils flared as his icy gaze narrowed on hers. He stared at her in silence for several beats, skimming her torso and face with his eyes before asking, "What are you offering, exactly?"

She swallowed, her entire body trembling with the vulnerability of her position. "Unlimited visitation. My support of you as her father." She inhaled sharply, the control she needed to feel slipping inexorably from her fingers. "Time with Emma alone."

"No." A feral light glinted in his blue eyes, and his expression telegraphed his triumph. "I want more."

Fear made her mouth go dry. "More?"

"I want you. At my disposal. In my bed. At my beck and call."

She sucked in a breath, her heart racing wildly within her chest. "You can't be serious!"

"Oh, but I am, sweet." His smile mocked her desperate circumstances. "You either marry me, or you become my mistress."

"I can't sleep with you again," she breathed. "You know I can't."

His arctic gaze glittered with brittle, dangerous threat. "And here I thought you were willing to do anything to keep Emma safe."

Stunned, she remained silent.

"You've done it before," he reminded her. "Quite willingly, if I recall."

Her stomach twisted beneath her ribs. "The situation is hardly the same now."

"Then you can marry me instead," came his curt reply.

He stood waiting before her, as immutable and stalwart as stone, while she grappled with a decision that wasn't a decision at all. She wanted to toss his counteroffer back in his face, to tell him there was *nothing* that would make her join him in his bed again. But the thought of Emma, a helpless, hurting pawn in this game of his, kept her silent. For Emma, for her sweet, innocent daughter…she'd sleep with the devil himself.

His eyes trapped hers, as impenetrable as granite, while icy fear slugged hard against her chest. "So what's it going to be? Marriage or my bed?"

"Do I really have a choice?"

He straightened and then rounded the hood of his car. "You have until tomorrow to decide."

CHAPTER EIGHT

When Colette entered the elevator to Stephen's office the following morning, she'd reached a decision. She wasn't convinced it was the right one, but given her options it was the best she could do.

The elevator doors slid open on his private floor and she approached his office with dread in her heart. She found him awaiting her arrival, looking well-rested and refreshed in a custom-made black suit. It was wretchedly unfair, especially since she felt like she'd spent the night inside a bread mixer set to high.

"You've reached your decision, I trust?" he asked, ushering her into his office and then closing the door behind them.

She lifted her chin and squared her shoulders, refusing to be cowed despite that fact that he'd backed her into a corner from which there was no escape. "You act as if there is a decision to be made. As if I have any choice in the matter."

"You do."

"Not really." She wouldn't show her fear, wouldn't reveal how scared she was to open herself up to the intimacy of his bed. But marriage wasn't an option. She would do anything to protect her sweet, innocent daughter from the anger and resentment of a loveless union. "You know I can't marry you," she said in a thin, defiant voice.

His grim smile held a veneer of triumph. "I'm sorry to hear that."

Anguished impotence, combined with her inability to avoid the coming pain, made her break out in a cold sweat. Her palms grew damp against her black tank dress, but she forced herself to maintain eye contact. The least she could do was hang on to her last shred of dignity. "No, you're not," she told him. "You're gloating."

"Do you blame me?"

She forced herself to breathe past the tightness in her chest. "No. I've lost. You've won. It's a heady feeling, I'm sure."

His triumphant eyes glimmered. "It is."

A wave of second thoughts she couldn't entertain clubbed within her veins. "Don't celebrate your victory just yet," she said in a reedy voice. "It's doubtful I'll make as good a mistress this time around."

"You underestimate your abilities, sweet." His blue eyes flashed with fiery heat as she swallowed back the retraction filling her throat. "Here. I have a gift for you," he said, withdrawing long enough to retrieve a package from the bottom drawer of his desk. Wrapped in distinctive white and silver paper, the gift bore the seal of New York's premier lingerie store.

"No." Panic clawed at her throat. She shook her head, her hands knotted against her waist as she backed away from him.

"Open it."

"No," she whispered. She stared at the package in mutinous fury, her stomach quivering in silent protest. "I don't want it."

He arched a brow. "Is this really how you intend to fulfill your mistress role? By defying me at every turn?"

"I don't want to be your mistress," she gasped. "I don't want your gifts. I don't want anything from you!"

The warmth in his eyes transformed to brittle ice. "You knew your choices," he said in a flat, commanding tone. "You chose this." His voice lowered ominously, overruling her arguments as he slid the package toward the edge of the desk. "Are you reneging already?"

Her voice wouldn't work. Her mouth felt dry as dust. So she shook her head jerkily and walked toward the package with shaking legs.

"Good girl," he said with a grim half-smile.

Swallowing, she slipped her trembling fingers beneath the tape as if approaching her own execution. By the time she'd finished opening the gift, her careful ministration leaving the paper completely unmarred, he'd moved to watch her from his chair behind the desk. Her hands stalled, hovering uncertainly above the delicate puddle of pale apricot silk and transparent lace.

"I bought it to match your freckles," he told her. "And your skin after I've pleasured you, when it's all flushed and pink."

Heat burned a path from her toes to her scalp.

"Come here." He beckoned her forward, between his chair and the edge of his desk.

She inched closer, her nervousness mounting with every step.

"That's right," he said as soon as she stood mere inches from his spread knees. "Now show it to me."

"I don't—"

"Show me."

She slowly twisted to withdraw the slippery film of silk, so thin and transparent she could have threaded the entire thing through a buttonhole. The doubled-up bodice was sheer enough to reveal the pattern of her fingerprints, and the thought of her breasts beneath the fine web of lace, exposed to his gaze, made a fine tremor claim her limbs.

"I can't wear this," she told him as she turned back to face him, her throat too tight to breathe.

"Of course you can."

"No." She shook her head, her mouth twisted into a distressed knot while pain cinched her lungs. "I agreed to be your mistress, to join you in your bed. But I never agreed to pretend I wanted to be there. Don't ask me to play the role of seductress when we both know it will be a lie."

"I'm willing to overlook a bit of acting."

"Stop it!" Desperate now, she flung the lingerie at his chest. It fluttered harmlessly to his lap, a smear of apricot trailing over the black silk of his suit pants.

"In case you've forgotten," he said, in voice of velvet overlaid with steel, "you've already played multiple roles for my pleasure. Roles we invented together. I've held and kissed your breasts, tasted your bare skin, and been close enough to smell the heat of your arousal." His eyes darkened. Flared as they trailed over her body. "Surely you recall when we—?"

"That was different," she interrupted while a torrent of unwanted memories raged through her. "I wanted to be there. I *wanted* to please you. It was my choice to be with you, and I always had the option to leave. I was in control."

"You were, weren't you?" he asked, rising from his seat while the apricot silk drifted down to puddle on the floor between them. He braced his palms beside her hips and leaned over her tipped face. "You set the boundaries. You chose the rules. While I, fool that I was, allowed it."

"We had a relationship of equals," she protested, terrified of this new shift in power.

"Did we?" A cool, mocking smile tugged against his mouth as he lifted his knuckles to stroke her jaw. "I seem to remember it differently. And, oddly enough, I suspect I'll like it more this time around."

"Well, I won't." Colette yanked free of his touch and tried to will the quaking from her limbs while her throat worked with her words. "And I won't pretend otherwise."

"We'll see," he said softly, leaning toward her until she had to arch her neck to keep his mouth from touching hers. "We'll see if I can change your mind, now that I'm the one in charge."

"You're not in charge," she challenged, and her eyes flashed with defiance. "You may direct my body, but you'll never direct me."

Stephen stared down at Colette's mutinous face, wondering how in the hell he'd gotten into this situation. Yes, he'd been angry at her and, yes, he'd wanted to hurt her for keeping Emma from him. He'd wanted to make her pay. But somehow, between their argument yesterday and their vows this morning, desire for her had diluted his desire for revenge.

"Shall I try to convince you otherwise?" he murmured. Giving in to the desire that had been tugging against his groin since he'd left her yesterday, he pressed up against the seam of Colette's gorgeous legs and brought his hands to her hips. "You might find that you can relinquish a bit of control and actually like it."

Her face flushed to the same delectable color of the lingerie he'd bought her and her gaze dipped to his lips. "I won't."

"Really?" His palms moved to cup the tight curve of her buttocks.

Her long, narrow hands pressed against his chest while she arched away from him, her mouth parting on an inhale. "I can't do this," she said, twisting within the confines of his hands. "I can't be your mistress. We have to come up with another compromise."

"Like what?" He stared at her mouth, that lush, kissable mouth, while one hand moved inexorably up along the silk spine of her dress and to the back of her arched neck. He wanted to taste every centimeter of her defiant, trembling softness, to explore the fine, delicate curve of her upper lip, to nip at the lush, petal-smooth swell of it until she moaned beneath him.

Just thinking of how she'd respond, he felt the hairs along his arms lift, priming him for the battle he fully intended to win.

She stared at him, her hazel eyes huge and alarmed within

her flushed face, while her hands shoved blindly at his shoulders. "Stephen—"

He caught her protest with his mouth, every last sense focused on the exquisite fit of her lips beneath his. For a moment neither of them moved. He allowed the feeling to wash over him, warm and heavy and so damned arousing he didn't know how his skin contained the desire swelling within.

He lingered at her lower lip for a moment, plying its softness with gentle, moist tugs before moving to her upper lip. When she softened beneath him, he touched his tongue to the delicate seam between them, urging her to open to him. To meet him with the same passion they'd shared once before. Stubborn minx that she was, she resisted. So he dragged his mouth from hers, tracking wet, raw kisses along the side of her neck until a haze of lust had him bending her backward within his arms.

God help him, he wanted to take her now, to spread her out before him on the virgin surface of his polished desk. He wanted to taste every glorious inch of her freckled skin, to chart the secrets of her intimate flesh until she came apart beneath his mouth and hands. Her body wanted it, too. She responded to him as he'd known she would, her fingers clinging helplessly to his shoulders, her thighs opening, welcoming, cradling his raging heat.

But then she was gone, his splayed hands gripping only air while a battering ram clamored for release between his legs. He lifted his head, staring at her with hooded eyes across the wide expanse of his desk. He felt drunk on Colette's drugging softness, and his chest caught on a shallow inhale. He could still taste her. Still hear her soft pants of desire, swift and urgent against his ear.

"You want this as much as I do."

"No," she lied, her gaze skittering away from his while her flushed cheeks and breasts and thighs told the truth. "I don't."

His expression was intense as he walked around the desk and then held her against the back of one of his armchairs. His hands, pressed tight against the base of her spine, were steely against her softness, the iron muscles of his thighs pressing heated awareness along her flesh despite the layers of clothing between them.

Low against her pelvis, she felt the hot, insistent pressure of his arousal, undeniable in its masculine quest for satisfaction. "Stephen," she gasped.

"Kiss me," he growled, his hips grinding against hers while a treacherous dampness gathered between her legs. "Kiss me and I'll consider a compromise."

"I already did." She closed her eyes, her own flesh joining in the challenge.

"No, sweet, *I* kissed *you*."

She remained silent as she turned her head to the side.

"If you're going to renege on your agreement, the least you can do is give me a decent parting kiss. A *real* kiss." He nudged his hips forward again and her insides clenched in helpless, desperate need. "Kiss me," he repeated in a rough voice, "and I'll agree to renegotiate without complaint."

"How do I know you aren't lying?" she heard herself say. She swallowed, cleared her throat, and tried to eliminate the husky note of arousal that had claimed her voice.

His thighs hardened to iron and she could see his nostrils flare as his gaze plundered hers. "You don't," he said in a silky, dangerous hum.

"But I should just kiss you anyway?"

Stephen abandoned her hands to tilt her face up to his perusal. "Yes."

"No," she said, feigning resolve despite her rising desire.

He simply stared at her, his breath stalling as he leaned forward and the tips of her breasts brushed the tight, flexed muscles of his chest. "Scared of how you'll respond?"

"Hardly." Slowly, she bit her lower lip, while his eyelids

drifted lower and her breasts grew heavy with weighted anticipation. She caught the scent of his skin, the warm combination of spice and salt she still smelled in her dreams.

"You're bluffing." he said with a degree of cockiness she should have hated, but didn't. "Shall I show you how I know?"

Trying to corral her own raging attraction to him, she regarded him with as much haughty dismissal as possible. "We're in your office."

"Never stopped you before," he reminded her.

She felt her face flush crimson. "In daylight. With your secretary just on the other side of that door."

Rather than reply, he shifted his hands to the zipper that started between her shoulderblades and traveled the length of her spine. Her breath caught in her throat as he lowered its slider with startling dexterity and speed. The tips of his fingers barely skimmed her quivering flesh, moving with swift, efficient concentration as he exposed her back in less time than it took for her to draw a protesting breath. She lifted her hands to her chest, keeping the bodice from falling forward and exposing her black demi-bra. But that left her back unprotected, and he took advantage of her lapse to drift his fingertips over the bare transition from waist to rib to bra, from spine to vulnerable neck.

She shivered while his fingers conspired with sunlight to flood her exposed flesh with heat. Goosebumps of awareness collected in all the places he continued to leave untouched. Unnerved, she squared her shoulders and held on to her bodice as if it were the last remaining protection she possessed. "This doesn't prove anything."

He ignored her as if she hadn't spoken, his fingers reaching up to withdraw the multiple pins from her upswept hair. Colette locked her knees and concentrated on drawing breath.

"I mean it," she said in a shaky voice, but he continued the silent, slow release of each pin until her hair finally listed and fell, its heavy weight settling against her back.

He reached for her hands next, prying them apart until she stood before him, her bodice listing forward and moving with her agitated breaths. He dipped his head until his mouth hovered over hers, so close she could feel the heated waft of his breath.

Awareness prickled along her skin, making the fine hairs on her arms and neck rise, and she swallowed against the moan that gathered in her throat. Closing her eyes, she willed herself to remain still. To win.

But how could she, when he'd stripped her of all her defenses? His hands trailed along the fragile wings of her collarbones. The soft brush of his fingers against her skin left her trembling, and she shuddered as his fingers drifted reverently over the tops of her breasts and then down and around her ribs to the open seam at the base of her spine. Knowing what he intended to do, knowing that soon she'd be fully exposed to his heated gaze, made her nipples constrict into near-painful points.

"Ready to kiss me yet?" he asked into the silence punctuated by their mingled breaths.

She wanted to shake her head, to force the denial through her parted lips, but her ability to speak had vanished along with her will. Paralyzed with desire, she simply stood without moving as he threaded his fingers beneath the opened vee at her back and pressed the black silk sheath down over her hips. Her dress crumpled to the floor about her ankles, leaving her clad only in her demi-bra, black heels, and transparent slip.

She shivered, and he lifted his hands back up to the sides of her neck, his thumbs trailing along the line of her jaw. He pressed against the thin ridge of bone, his touch demanding and soothing at the same time. Strong fingers tunneled through her hair, dragging a low moan up to her throat as he massaged her scalp. She wanted to arch up against him, to give in to the temptation to fling her arms around his wide shoulders and haul him close.

He stroked lower, his thumbs manipulating the tight muscles at the sides of her neck and the twin aches at the joint between neck and shoulder. Pain and delight merged, drowning her in sensation and a heavy desire for more. More. His mouth dropped to her ear to whisper, the hum of breath and sound eliciting a shiver that collected in a poignant ache at the tips of her breasts.

"Tell me you want this, Colette."

She bit her lip and closed her eyes, words still out of reach.

A low huff of laughter caressed the side of her neck. "Still stubborn as ever, I see."

He stood close enough that she could feel his erection, thick and insistent, against her belly. Knowing that she aroused him left her feeling slightly drunk, more than a little dizzy, and scared. Scared that she'd lose her heart to him all over again. His fingertips had drifted from her neck to graze soft circles around the tight knot of her straining nipple.

Colette sucked her lips between her teeth and tried to keep from crying out. She wanted to snatch his wrist and pull his palm hard against her aching breast. Embarrassed by how easily he'd dismantled her defenses, she closed her eyes and willed her traitorous body into submission. Until a few seconds later, her held breath was expelled in a rush when he dipped his fingers beneath the cup of her bra, lifting her breast within his warm, waiting hand.

"Colette," he breathed, and her heart stuttered to a standstill as he bent his head to press his hot mouth against her puckered flesh. Trembles claimed her legs, stealing her balance and forcing her to sway against him for support. Beneath her shaking fingers, his shoulders felt like boulders.

His other hand shoved at the silky hem of her slip, revealing her bare thighs her to his fingers. She heard his fractured breathing change tempo, felt the tremor in his hand as he delved between lace and silk and skin to cup her heat for one dizzying moment. Then he withdrew his hand and reached for her knee, spreading and lifting and positioning her with mind-numbing ease.

A belated sense of modesty compelled her to press against his chest, to close her legs and cross an arm over her exposed breasts as he efficiently lifted her, carried her, and then deposited her on the soft, supple seat of the chair. Panic tinged with excitement arrowed through her—did he plan to seduce her here? Now?

Struggling to sit upright, she adjusted her flimsy slip and clamped her knees together.

Squatting before her, he drew her hands aside with surprising gentleness and then redirected them back to the supple armrests of his chair. "Don't," he said. "I want to see you."

She swallowed, not fighting him as he removed her shoes and then slid the black silk of her slip back up her thighs. Flames of desire suffused every inch of her skin. She could taste her longing and the awful awareness of how much she'd missed him, how much she'd missed *this*.

Balanced on the balls of his feet, his powerful legs bent at the knee, he stared at her, and she could do little but stare back. Sunlight gilded the tips of his black hair and cool air conditioning filtered over her torso. Subtle sounds layered beneath the quietness of their joint solitude…the persistent drone of Manhattan traffic, the muffled ebb and flow of hotel elevators, the distant blare of horns and emergency sirens. But here, cloaked in nothing but air and sunlight and silk, it felt like the world had constricted to contain just the two of them. Alone.

Light-headed and confused, Colette remained pliant and unresisting as he touched her, his hands sliding up from her knees in a slow, deliberate ascent. A tremor gained ground, making her thighs tremble as he reached the transition from flesh to elastic and damp black satin. His fingers brushed the

silky panel between her legs and a small whimper of longing lodged in her throat. And then his hands continued north,
until he threaded his fingers beneath the waistband of her
underwear, lifted her, and then skillfully peeled the scrap of
satin down over the rounded curve of her buttocks.

He sank back onto his heels and watched her face as he
continued to remove her panties. Warm fingers skimmed the
outside of her thighs, the backs of her knees and her trembling calves, until he'd disrobed her of every stitch of clothing but her bra and her slip. Her toes curled against the plush
carpeting and he reached to wrap his fingers around her vulnerable ankle. Slowly, he drew her feet wide, planting them
beside his spread thighs. He moved to her knees next, his
warm hands pressing them open beneath his intense gaze.
His nostrils flared and his eyes darkened with arousal as his
attention dipped.

Exposed, open, and flooded with a damp, yearning heat,
she swallowed against the searing touch of his gaze upon her
shadowed flesh. A sweet, shocked tremor of embarrassment
and desire leaked through her chest, making it difficult to
breathe. She knotted her hands against the supple leather of
his chair, gripping the edge of the armrests while he stared
at her. She remembered how he'd looked at her every time
they'd made love, as if there were no one in his world but her.
She could read his arousal in the huge, hard bulge between
his legs, in the darkened crests of his cheeks and glittering
eyes. And for the first time in over five years she felt beautiful. Wanted.

The tip of his index finger trailed northward from her knee,
creating a path of heat as he moved up her pale, twitching
thigh. "You're so soft," he told her in a low voice.

"It's my lotion," she said inanely.

A small smile tugged at one side of his mouth and the rest
of his fingers joined the first. She sucked in a breath as he

gently transcribed circles upon her flesh. "You smell good, too."

She bit her lip as his long, tanned hands moved over her skin, inching higher and higher with every pass. When he brushed the juncture of her thighs, her breath stopped altogether. She wanted to press up against his fingers, to relieve the building tension that had her squirming and panting and wanting. Needing. And with the realization of her need she knew, as surely as she knew her own dreams, that if he made love to her now she'd lose herself entirely. Permanently. Only this time, she wouldn't be strong enough to survive his rejection when it came.

"Stop," she said with her last vestige of self-preservation. Gripping his wrists, she pressed his fingers away from the ache that clamored for release, from the silvery surge of heat that begged her to reconsider. "Stop," she repeated in a shaky voice.

Her words didn't penetrate at first. His taut focus was so centered on the shadowed evidence of her arousal that her meaning didn't register for a long, interminable second. When it did, he felt like he'd swallowed broken glass.

She said stop. Stephen bit down against his back teeth, his fingers pressing hard against her thighs.

Stop.

She meant it this time. He could hear the panicked conviction in her tone. So he would stop. Even if it killed him, he would do the impossible. He sucked in a ragged inhale and closed his eyes, the sight of the long, freckled thighs spread before him begging him to forget civility and ravage her despite her protests. The sweet scent of her desire, the flush of arousal that turned her skin pink beneath the sunlight, the small whimpering sounds she made when he touched her… All of it fired a burn of need so desperate he didn't know how he managed to contain the beast within. Every cell burned to devour her, to bite and suck and taste and consume until the flavors and textures of Colette were branded into his brain.

His breath hissed between his teeth as he slowly forced his fingers from her flesh. One more moment of touching her, of smelling her and watching her, and he'd explode.

Slowly, painfully, he stood and turned, his focus so blurred he had to grope for balance against the edge of his desk. Bracing his hands against its polished surface, he dropped his head between his hunched shoulders and concentrated on collecting what remained of his self-control. "Get dressed," he told her between clenched teeth. "Or I won't be responsible for what happens."

He heard her rustling behind him, fumbling for her discarded clothing. He closed his eyes while he focused on his breathing. In. Out. He could still smell her, the salty, musky aroma of her flesh. He wanted to bury his face between her rosy breasts, to inhale her heat until she moaned and arched up beneath him.

"I'm sorry," she said after a few torturous minutes. Her voice sounded small. "I didn't—"

"Don't!" he interrupted harshly. "Don't apologize."

Figuring it was safe, he turned to find her hair mussed and her skin flushed that lovely, kissable pink. He knotted his hands against the urge to haul her close again, to finish what they'd started.

No. Though he knew he could overrule her wishes and seduce her body into compliance, he found he wanted more than control, more than being in charge. He wanted *her*. Willing, pliant, and beneath him because she *wanted* to be there of her own volition. Suddenly the obligation he'd forced upon her tasted like ash in his mouth, and he had no appetite for it anymore.

His own arousal aside, he had to take her home, out of arms' reach. Away from him. "Don't think this is over."

She exhaled unsteadily. "I won't."

Swallowing back the desire that still clubbed within his chest and made his suit feel ten sizes too small, he adjusted his jacket and then collected his keys from his desk. He snagged the negligee from the floor as well, stuffing it deep into his pocket.

"Is Emma at home?" he asked, making his uncomfortable way to the open door.

"Why?"

"We're going to tell her I'm her father."

"Now?" she asked in a high, panicked voice.

"Yes. Now. She's my daughter. It's time she knew it."

CHAPTER NINE

EMMA must have seen their arrival through the window, because she'd already pushed the screen door open before they'd finished climbing the porch steps. She wore a voluminous yellow gown that Stephen thought looked a little the worse for wear, making her look like a bedraggled fairy plucked from a picture book.

"Momma!" she hollered, launching herself at Colette's waist with undisguised glee. "You're home!"

Colette staggered a bit for balance, one arm flying up to wrap about Emma's back while her free hand shot out to grip the handrail. Stephen reached to press a steadying hand at the small of Colette's back, and she immediately stiffened away from his touch. "Hello, sweetheart," she said, dipping to press a kiss against their daughter's tousled head. "Have you been a good girl this morning?"

The grinning mite nodded enthusiastically. "I drawed a picture and me an' Janet maked lemonade. From scratch!" she crowed, a budding chef who'd obviously internalized her mother's exacting standards for freshness.

"You remember Mr. Whitfield, don't you?"

Emma cocked her golden head, her blue eyes tracking his features with undisguised interest. "'Course. Momma's your en...your em..." Her tiny rosebud mouth puckered as she tried to recall the word. "What'd you say she was?"

She was supposed to be my mistress. "My employee?"

Emma beamed and nodded her head. "Yes, your employee. An' you like princesses with blue eyes."

A queer rush of possessiveness gripped his chest as he stared down at his daughter. How had he not recognized her as his from the very first? "Yes, I do."

"Sweetheart," Colette interrupted as she moved up to the top step and reached for the door. "Why don't we go inside and fetch Mr. Whitfield some of that lemonade you made? He and I have something important to tell you."

"'Kay, but we hafta make more," she said as she turned to skip past her mother. "Me and Janet drinked it all."

He and Colette trailed inside after their daughter, her excited chatter informing Janet of their arrival. "Let me do the talking," Colette murmured beneath her breath.

Resenting her claim of control yet again, he felt irritation coil in his chest. "Why? So you can spin it in your favor?"

"So I can spin it in *hers*," she hissed. "I want to minimize her shock and confusion."

"There wouldn't be any shock or confusion if you'd—"

"I know that," she snapped, turning to face him with her hands knotted at her thighs. She checked over her shoulder and then lowered her voice. "But it doesn't change the reality of here and now. She doesn't know you are her father yet, and we can't just spring it on her without taking time to prepare her."

"Prepare her?" he asked, arching a brow.

She scowled, a trapped lioness protecting her cub. "She's a *child*, Stephen, a sweet, innocent child, and telling her will require a bit more sensitivity than you possess."

He felt himself bristle beneath the insult. "I can be—"

"You can't."

Scanning her mulish expression and the lines of worry around her hazel eyes, he realized with a sudden lurch in his gut that she was scared. Despite his anger and frustration, he felt something within him soften and shift. And, even though she deserved everything he saw fit to inflict, he decided it wouldn't kill him to exhibit a little mercy. He could grant her this small modicum of control. "Fine. You do the talking. I won't intervene."

Her shoulders slumped with her relief. "Thank you."

"But you owe me for this," he said, reminding her that his capitulation came at a cost.

A flush climbed her face while her eyes flashed. "Fine. I owe you. Add it to my tab."

Her tab. As if she ever intended to pay. He scowled, wishing he was merciless enough to exploit this new role of creditor to its fullest.

Now that the moment was upon them, Colette didn't know quite how to feel. Nervous, jittery and scared, she couldn't begin to predict how Emma would react.

Trepidation filled her lungs as she entered her bright yellow and blue kitchen to find Emma on her knees atop a kitchen stool, helping Janet squeeze fresh lemons into a pitcher. Colette's heart twisted painfully but she persevered, donning a cheerful smile and a somewhat steady voice. "Janet," she began, "would you mind excusing us for an hour or so?"

Her nanny arched curious gray brows, her gaze skipping from Colette to Stephen to Emma and then back again. "Of course not, dear. Is there anything—?"

"No, I'm fine," Colette interrupted.

They stood awkwardly, a silent tableau of untold secrets, until Janet blurted, "I'll just pick some things up at the deli, then. And catch up with Helen. It's been a while since we've had a good talk."

"Thank you," Colette said as Janet collected her purse and then bustled out the back door.

Colette waited until Janet disappeared from sight before pulling out one of her three chairs and gingerly lowering herself into it. "Emma, sweetheart, why don't you come sit on Momma's lap?"

Emma must have sensed that something momentous was afoot, because her eyes widened momentarily before she climbed down off the stool and came to stand before Colette's bent knees. "What about your lemonade?"

"We can have it later." She reached for her daughter's sturdy little torso and lifted her up onto her thighs. "Mr. Whitfield and I have something important to tell you first. Remember?"

Emma's blue gaze, so like her father's, skipped to where Stephen now sat, across from their scarred kitchen table. "Uh-huh."

"Do you remember that Momma used to live in a place called England before she had you?"

"Like Mr. Whitfield?"

"Yes, just like Mr. Whitfield. And when I lived there Mr. Whitfield and I…we were friends."

Emma stared at Colette, her expression curious and not at all alarmed. "Is he still your friend?"

I doubt it. "Yes, sweetheart. He is. And he wants to be your friend, too." Colette felt her stomach pitch as Emma's compact body twisted to look at her father. "Would that be all right with you?"

"You wanna have play dates with me?" she asked, her small brow furrowing.

His eyelashes flickered for an instant, betraying a nervousness she'd have thought him incapable of feeling and sending a sharp lurch through her chest. "Absolutely," he answered with a smile, and his blue eyes were filled with a tenderness Colette had never seen before. "But only if you want me to."

She paused for a second, studying Stephen where he sat. "Do you have prince clothes?"

"Prince clothes?"

"For Beauty and the Beast."

He cocked his brow at that, a disarmed smile tugging at his mouth. "Do you think I'm a beast, Emma?"

The trill of her giggle diluted some of the tension in the room as she nodded. "'Course I do! You're gigantic!"

"In that case, I think I can probably come up with some prince clothes." He angled a look at Colette. "Do you think a tuxedo would suffice?"

"Yes," she said, smiling despite herself. Hauling in a stabilizing breath, and praying that her voice held steady, Colette brought the conversation back to the topic at hand. "Emma?"

Emma looked over her shoulder at Colette. "What?"

She tried to keep her hands from tightening too much about Emma's body. "It turns out that Mr. Whitfield here is more than just a friend." She offered a comforting smile. "To us, at least."

Curiosity lit her baby's eyes. "He is?"

"Yes. Mr. Whitfield is…" Her smile lost a bit of its moorings as she lifted shaking fingers to brush back a wayward curl from Emma's upturned face. "Mr. Whitfield is your daddy."

Emma stared at her with wondering eyes, her expression slowly transforming from curiosity to surprise. "My daddy?"

"Yes."

She turned back to Stephen. "You're my *daddy*?"

"I am." His deep voice held none of Colette's unsteadiness, but she could detect the note of emotion underlying the words nonetheless.

"But Momma said my daddy lived far, far away," she said.

Colette fingered the soft curls at Emma's neck and answered. "He used to. He lived in England for a long, long time. But now he's here," said Colette. "And he's very excited to have you as his little girl."

Emma nodded slowly, processing this new development in her small, insulated world. "Is he gonna take us to live in England now?"

Colette ran a reassuring hand down Emma's back. "No, sweetheart. We'll stay right here, just like we always have."

"And he's gonna live in our house?" she asked.

"No, he'll have his own house," she rushed to answer before Stephen could. "But he'll visit lots of times, and maybe you can visit him sometimes, too. Would you like that?"

Emma cocked her head, her expression skeptical. "Is your house far away?"

"I live at the hotel where your momma works right now, but maybe you can help me pick out new place to live. One that has a special room just for you."

"Can you get a castle?"

He smiled and exchanged a quick glance with Colette. "I don't know if there are any castles nearby, but we could certainly look."

"'Kay."

He leaned back to withdraw a small box from his suit pocket. "I've brought a present for you as well, if your momma says it's all right for you to have it."

Emma gasped and immediately turned to Colette. "Can I?"

Colette's heart skipped a beat as she nodded, realizing she'd opened the door to losing her little girl to a parent with more money, more toys, and the ability to fulfill every material wish in a way she never could. "Of course you can, sweetheart."

Stephen nudged the white jewelry box across the table toward Emma, who in turn exclaimed with pleasure before pulling off the pink bow and grappling with the lid. She resisted Colette's offer to help, her childish efforts notching her brow and catching her tongue between her teeth. When she finally figured out the hinges at the back, it was with undisguised pride in her own abilities that she opened the box and peered inside.

Emma, who normally had a comment for everything, was rendered momentarily speechless.

"Oh, look," said Colette, her chest tightening as she leaned sideways to see the delicate gold chain and pendant nestled within. "It's a necklace."

Emma nodded soundlessly, her blue eyes wide and shining.

"It's very beautiful, don't you think?"

She arched back to whisper in Colette's ear. "It's a princess necklace!" she divulged in an excited puff of warm breath. "With a crown on it!"

It was the perfect gift, exquisitely perfect, in fact, and Colette lifted blurring eyes to gauge Stephen's reaction. He was watching their daughter, his smile uncharacteristically uncertain around the edges.

"What do you say?" she prompted Emma.

Emma gasped in belated recollection of her manners, and then launched herself off Colette's lap. Before Colette had registered her intent, Emma had raced around the table and wrapped her arms as far as they could reach around Stephen's chair and waist. "Thank you, Daddy! Thank you!"

For a beat of silence Stephen's surprised gaze held Colette's, before he leaned sideways to return Emma's hug. "You're welcome, sweet," he said before clearing his throat. "Do you want me to help you put it on?"

Emma nodded her enthusiasm, placed the box in his broad palm, and then swung to present her back, lifting her curls and tipping her head forward without a moment's hesitation.

Once he'd fastened the clasp, she lifted her chin and fingered the tiny gold and pearl crown. "Do I look like a princess, Momma?" she asked.

Colette blinked back her tears and nodded while Stephen answered in a gruff voice, "You don't just look like a princess, you *are* a princess."

* * *

"I wouldn't have thought it possible, but I think you managed to find the only modern-day castle within a hundred miles of New York," Colette observed three weeks later as Stephen welcomed them into the new home he'd purchased in the East Hamptons. With its long halls of checkered marble, heavy chandeliers, dual curved staircases, and an entry foyer that could accommodate the entire New York Senate, it was large enough to host state balls of fairytale proportions.

"I promised our little princess a castle, and I always deliver on my promises," Stephen answered as he offered his hand to their daughter. "Emma, would you like to see the movie theater or the indoor pool first?"

"Yes!" she answered, reaching for his outstretched hand and jumping forward to stand by his denim-clad thigh. "C'mon, Momma!"

Emma, more excited than Colette had ever seen her, skipped alongside Stephen as he led them on a tour of each wing of the colonial mansion. He showed them a six-car garage, countless bedrooms, a giant gourmet kitchen, and multiple entertaining rooms of various sizes while Emma exclaimed over every new discovery.

"Can we play hide 'n' seek?" she asked, after they'd explored the extensive exterior grounds.

"Maybe later," answered Colette. "Right now, I'm worried you'd get lost and I'd never find you." Dressed in a caramel-colored wrap skirt, blue oxford and espadrilles, Colette had trailed behind Stephen and Emma for the entire tour, feeling inexplicably tense. Colette's tiny home would have fit inside Stephen's a good dozen times, and the sheer size of the place overwhelmed her. Though it was beautiful beyond Colette's wildest imaginings, it reminded her of a fantasy getaway, or a mausoleum she doubted could ever feel like a real home.

Emma, on the other hand, thought it was perfect, and she spent the next half-hour rushing pell-mell down the interior hallways, exploring nooks and crannies and investigating the maze of cupboards beneath the stairs.

Colette would have thought watching a small child explore with no particular destination in mind would have bored Stephen to distraction, but it hadn't. He was proving to be a wonderful father to Emma: kind, patient, and involved. In fact, if she were honest with herself, he was everything she'd hoped he might be with their daughter.

So why wasn't she happier about it?

And why, like now, when he looked at her with those blue eyes of his, did her every cell seem to come alive with yearning? Ever since she'd called a halt to their lovemaking that fateful day in his office, he'd stopped trying to seduce her. He talked to her only about Emma or hotel business, and avoided being alone with her at all costs. He hadn't mentioned marriage again, and he seemed to have forgotten all about his requirement that she be his mistress.

While Colette, to her eternal consternation, found herself unable to think of anything else.

It was because he was too handsome, she thought dizzily. His black hair, gleaming with blue lights no matter the weather, begged to be smoothed back from his broad forehead. His hands and forearms, bronzed and muscular beneath rolled white cuffs, and his powerful legs encased in worn denim, created a heady combination of male virility that had her eyes darting to the unmistakable bulge between his thighs.

Heat scalded Colette's cheeks as she dragged her attention back to his chin. How was she supposed to think clearly with him looking the way he did?

With him looking at *her* the way he did?

She felt the weight of his stare on her face, the hungry gaze that seemed to track her movements whenever they happened to be in the same room. Knowing he wanted her, yet had no intention of acting on his desire, made her insides twist up in nervousness. In longing. In a wholly inappropriate, unwelcome desire to touch. To feel. To forget all the reasons things could never work between them and simply start anew.

She told herself she should be glad he hadn't pushed for more, that he no longer touched her. That when he tired of playing at being a father and left, she'd be grateful that they hadn't slept together.

She would be.

Several hours later, after a swim and a movie, they retired to Stephen's private dining room for dinner. The three of them sat at one corner of an impossibly long mahogany table and ate grilled steaks, seasoned new potatoes, and fresh green beans grown in his new estate gardens. Household staff appeared and disappeared soundlessly while Emma chatted about all the things she planned to do during her future sleepovers.

After they'd finished, and their plates had been cleared away, Colette collected the dessert she'd brought from home. "Do you want ice cream with your pastry?" she asked Stephen, her spoon poised over a fresh carton of vanilla bean.

"Don't I always?" he answered.

Colette scooped a hearty portion of both ice cream and fruit tart onto his plate and then leaned to assist Emma with the finishing touches. "That's right," she said, her hand curved around Emma's. "You drizzle the strawberry sauce over the whole thing, first this way and then...that. Perfect!" She grinned at Emma and then lifted the dessert for Stephen's inspection. "What do you think? It's Emma's first homemade fruit tart."

"It looks delicious," Stephen said.

"It's my favorite," Emma told him as she readied her drizzling spoon for the next serving. "Momma let me roll the dough all by myself."

"Did she now?" His gaze snagged on Colette's and a reminiscent smile eased its way across his face. "She taught me how to make my favorite dessert, too. Only mine was black and white mousse cake."

Colette sucked in a breath, remembering the first time she'd tried to teach him that unique blend of almond, chocolate, cream and ganache. He'd watched her until she'd finished her explanation, his eyes tracking her like a lazy cat's, and then demanded to lick the bowl. Except he'd spread the leftovers on her flesh before he'd done any licking at all. Her nipples tingled at the erotic memory of his mouth at her breast, tasting her. Consuming her.

"Maybe you can make that next time?" he asked.

Colette's face heated and she immediately shifted her focus to the ice cream between her hands. "Sure," she mumbled, grateful that Emma was in the room to corral her impulses.

Later, after Emma's bath and a lengthy debate over which princess nightgown would go best with her new pink-canopied bed, she was finally ready for her first sleepover at Daddy's. Colette lifted Emma up to her high mattress and helped her climb beneath the covers.

"Do you get to sleep over, too?" Emma asked.

Colette's hands stalled and the heat of Stephen's gaze upon her profile made her skin flush. "No, sweetheart," she said, tugging the blankets high and tucking them beneath Emma's arms. "Momma has her own bed at home, remember?"

"Maybe Daddy can give you one of his so you can have two beds like me!"

Rather than continue a discussion she didn't care to have, Colette dug in her bag for Emma's favorite storybook. "Would you like me to read to you before lights out?" she asked.

After Emma had listened to her favorite fairytale twice, read once by Colette and once again by Stephen, Emma drifted off to sleep in her high bed, a golden-haired angel dressed in yellow and pink.

"Thank you for letting her stay," Stephen said quietly.

"She's talked of nothing else for days," she admitted.

They stood looking down at the sweet curve of Emma's cheek and curled fist, neither of them speaking for several seconds.

"I think she likes the house," he finally whispered.

"You think?" Colette shook her head, a small smile tugging at her mouth. "If you keep spoiling her like this," she warned, "she'll be impossible at thirteen."

"We'll deal with that when the time comes," he answered in a low voice.

Colette turned to face him, stunned anew that he planned to be around for Emma's adolescence. That the permanence of fatherhood didn't seem to deter him at all. "You're good with her," she said softly. "Better than I expected."

"You do tend to underestimate me, don't you?" he answered, without lifting his gaze from their slumbering child.

She didn't answer, uncomfortably aware that he probably spoke the truth.

"I've always liked children," he continued, leaning to draw the blanket up over Emma's curved shoulder. "And Emma's particularly easy to like." His big palm cupped the back of her head before he straightened and strode silently toward the door.

He exited the room without another word, and Colette felt her perceptions of him shift yet again. After watching him with Emma, his harsh edges softened by the incongruity of a child at his knee and a doll in his hand, she could no longer cast him in the role she'd formerly assigned to him.

For beneath the veneer of international playboy and ruthless businessman lurked a layer she'd never suspected. A layer Emma could rely on and trust.

A layer perhaps she could trust as well.

CHAPTER TEN

STEPHEN could hear Colette behind him as she closed Emma's door with a soft click. Uncomfortable with the frustrated desire he always, always felt for her, he strode down the muffled carpet of the hall toward the staircase. Though he'd been able to keep himself in check these past few weeks, doing so had proven to be a special kind of hell.

No torture the Whitfield family had ever devised came close to the hours he'd spent with Colette without touching her. Without kissing her.

"Where'd you learn to interact with children?" she asked, stopping a couple of treads above the base of the staircase.

He turned to find her face at eye level with his, far closer than he'd anticipated. A few strands of hair had slipped their moorings to curl around her jaw, and the urge to tuck them back into the neat coil at her nape roared through him with the force of a hurricane.

Knowing that he didn't dare touch her sent a sharp spike of irritation through his gut and sharpened his tone. "Why? Because a man like me shouldn't know the first thing about how to behave around his own daughter?"

Her eyes widened in surprise while her skin blushed a soft, delectable pink. "I didn't mean it that way," she protested.

Feeling unreasonable, and not caring, he bit out, "No? Then how *did* you mean it, exactly?"

"Don't bark at me for being curious, Stephen." Her hand

had tightened against the banister, her knuckles and finger-tips white even though her voice remained calm. Oh, yes. That was his Colette. Eternally in control and calm. It made him want to shout at her, to shake her, to kiss her until ragged emotions made her hands and voice and flesh tremble. "Some men can be uncomfortable around kids," she continued, un-aware of the firestorm of longing, of pure, unadulterated *want* simmering beneath the surface of his skin. "And the world knows that caring for a child is hardly innate for a man who spends all his time—"

"I'm not that kind of man," he snapped.

Though she stiffened, she didn't back down. "It still doesn't mean you've had experience with children."

He glared at her for a moment, before biting out, "My mum's family is big. Dozens of cousins all over the place, and most of them with a couple of kids apiece. Between holidays and Sunday dinners spent tending children while the adults gossiped, I probably have more experience than you."

She stared at him, her mouth slightly parted and her eyes wide with shock.

"What?" he sneered. "Not convinced? Shall I tell you about all the nappies I changed, the bottles I heated, the—?"

"No," she rushed to say. "It's just…I have a hard time pic-turing you as the family nanny."

"Only because you can't see beyond your own prejudices," he ground out.

"I don't—"

"You do. You look at me and see a playboy." Defensiveness and righteous anger flared hot within his chest. "A selfish, self-centered man incapable of commitment or fatherhood."

"No," she protested. "I don't. Not anymore. I mean, I did at first, but I'm beginning to realize I never really knew you at all."

"And whose fault is that?" he asked.

When she stared at him, stunned and silent, he turned on

his heel and strode toward the wing that housed his master suite.

"Certainly not mine!" she finally blurted, clambering down the remaining steps and hurrying after him. "You're the one who never told me anything about yourself beyond the most superficial of details!"

He stopped at the door to his bedroom, turning to face her with fury tightening his lungs. "Would you have been interested if I had?"

She stiffened as if he'd slapped her. "How can you even ask such a thing?"

"Oh, I don't know." He leaned over her until she arched her neck to maintain the distance between them. He could see the fragile beat of the pulse in the side of her neck, the dilated pupils of her wide, distressed eyes. Knowing he'd disconcerted her made him viciously, irrationally glad. "It could be that talk about *your* past was strictly off-limits," he reminded her in a low, menacing voice. "Or have you conveniently forgotten about your demand for no commitments, no strings, and no questions?"

She pressed her mouth shut to conceal its faint hint of trembling.

"You wanted nothing beyond hours of mind-altering sex and culinary abandon," he continued cruelly. "Which I provided. Without complaint."

A crimson blush streaked northward from her neck. "We didn't share a child then."

The air between them heated with his frustration, his banked arousal, and an anger he didn't dare analyze. "Are you telling me that now we have Emma you're suddenly going to tell me all about your past and answer all of my questions?"

Hazel eyes flared in alarm before she shuttered them behind a sweep of lashes. "Is that what you want?"

I want a hell of a lot more than that, sweet. "You can't even stomach the idea of kissing me again. Why would I be foolish enough to think you'll answer questions you'd never answer before?"

"Because it's your right to know about the mother of your child." She swallowed, her hazel eyes filled with a dizzying combination of guilt and fear. "You deserve to ask any question you want, no matter how difficult it might prove for me to answer."

Her response slugged him like a hammer to the chest. "You don't mean that," he finally said.

"I do."

He stared at her without speaking for several long seconds, her offer hanging suspended between them like a white flag of truce when he'd expected nothing but more walls and more weapons.

"Do you still see them?" she ventured, breaking the silence. "The cousins you tended?"

His jaw bunched and he averted his eyes, torn between the dual desires to glean information about Colette and keep the details of his own past buried. "No," he said flatly.

"No?" She dipped to study his downturned face. "Why not?"

He lifted his chin and answered, his face and voice carefully blank. "After my parents died, my father's family sent me to boarding school. It didn't provide much opportunity for visiting." And the rare days that were allocated for family visits had been, for him at least, achingly empty. He still remembered how alone and lost he'd felt, how he'd waited in the receiving room with his heart in his throat while he watched happy boys reunite with their adoring families. He remembered every Friday, when the post delivered gifts and cookies and newsy letters from home to everyone but him. Separate, forgotten and abandoned, he'd sworn never to need anyone ever again.

"Your parents died?" Colette asked, ripping his thoughts back to the present. "How? What happened?"

He'd spare her the details of his mother's death and his father's subsequent despair. "It was an accident."

She reached for his taut forearm, her cool fingers like a brand upon his flesh. "I'm so sorry, Stephen. No one should have to endure a loss like that when they're a child."

He looked at her hand without moving. "I survived," he said in an even tone, while deep, deep within the small boy he'd kept hidden from the world howled out his agreement.

"Of course you did," she rushed to assure him. "How old were you?"

"Eleven."

Her grip upon his arm tightened. "And your family sent you to boarding school? Alone?"

"Oh, there were plenty of Whitfield cousins there," he said tightly, remembering anew the myriad tortures the more acceptable Whitfields had chosen to inflict upon him. "They went out of their way to make me feel...*welcome*."

"What did they do to you?" she whispered.

He smiled, concealing the pain and resentment and buried hurt he refused to feel anymore. "Besides hate me and accuse me of stealing what they felt belonged to them? Nothing worth mentioning."

"Nothing worth mentioning?" she gasped in outrage. "You were eleven!"

"True. But age doesn't really matter when money's involved, does it?" he asked as he disengaged his arm from her fingers.

"Money?" Her brow pleated with confusion and she stepped toward him, reaching for his withdrawn wrist. "Are you talking about the Whitfield Grand?"

For the first time ever, he avoided her touch. The note of concern in her voice was stinging the raw wounds of his past. "Of course. I own half the family hotel and they think I shouldn't own any of it at all."

"But why wouldn't you be entitled to your share? You're a Whitfield just as much as your cousins!"

"You'd certainly think so, wouldn't you?" he said.

When she looked at him as if she wanted to pry deeper, to delve beneath the layers of hatred and revenge he'd carried for twenty-five years, he pushed his door open and stepped into his master suite, leaving her to follow if she dared.

Mustering her courage, Colette stepped in after him, suddenly feeling like an interloper in the navy and brown space that held not a hint of feminine softness. Though he'd answered every one of her questions, she couldn't shake the impression that he was hiding something from her. It felt as if, despite his claims, he didn't want her peering beneath his surface to the hidden hurts he kept locked away from the world. Hurts she knew they had to discuss if they were ever to move forward as parents for Emma.

"Is that why they didn't let you see your mother's family anymore? Because they were worried about the influence they might have over you?"

His eyes flashed, a lightning strike of vulnerability that vanished as quickly as it appeared. "The O'Fallons didn't want anything to do with the Whitfields after my mother died." His jaw flexed. "Especially me."

"But that doesn't make any sense." She shook her head, her heart pinching at the image of Stephen abandoned and alone. "You were all they had left of your mother and I'm sure they loved you. There had to have been some sort of misunderstanding. Have you tried contacting any of them?"

"No. And I won't." He turned his back on her and stalked farther into the room.

Her breath caught in her lungs, fear and pity and an urge to soothe him warring within her chest. No wonder he was so driven to create a family for Emma. He didn't want his daughter to feel alone the way he had.

A fresh wave of guilt over the time with Emma she'd stolen

from him brought a lump to her throat. "I'm sorry I didn't tell you about Emma before."

He went utterly still.

"It was wrong of me to keep her from you the way I did."

Slowly, he turned to face her, his gaze delving into hers. "Why the change of opinion?"

She swallowed. "I didn't think you'd want her. I was wrong."

"Why on earth wouldn't a father want his own child?"

Opening a window to her past that she'd always kept sealed shut terrified her, but she could no longer rationalize keeping her past buried. Stephen deserved to know why she'd kept Emma from him. She couldn't expect him to trust her if she wasn't willing to trust him in turn. So she hauled in a deep breath and confessed the truth that had shaped her entire life.

"My father didn't want me," she said. Before she could see pity on his face, she rushed to finish. "And, because of that, I believed you'd react the same way he did. I was wrong and I'm sorry." Having divulged the reason for her reticence, she turned on her heel and strode back the way she'd come.

He stopped her withdrawal with a firm hand upon her elbow. Slowly, inexorably, he circled her until he faced her. "Your father didn't want you?"

She forced herself to meet his eyes, feigning a strength she didn't feel while her throat worked with the confession. "I was a burden he didn't want, and the only reason he and my mother married."

A hint of anger stole across his features. "Surely they didn't tell you that?"

"They didn't have to. They were miserable, and wouldn't have been if I hadn't been born."

His nostrils flared while he regarded her in silence. After a taut moment, he asked, "How old were you when you figured this out?"

"I overheard them arguing about me when I was eight."

Dropping his gaze to her mouth, he inhaled. Exhaled. And then raised his eyes back to hers. "It wasn't your fault," he told her fiercely.

Colette knotted her hands at her sides, hating the fact that they were trembling. Hating the fact that she felt so exposed. "My mother said as much, but I knew it was just to keep from hurting my feelings. I wasn't blind. I knew my father hated her for getting pregnant and forcing him into marriage."

The back of her nose burned as she remembered the way she'd tried so hard to be the perfect daughter, her hair neatly braided and her skinned knees hidden behind tight white socks. She'd wanted a daddy who loved her so badly.

"I knew he hated me." She blinked back the stupid, stupid film of tears that had gathered and lifted her chin as if her father's rejection no longer bothered her. "And I never wanted Emma to feel that way. I was afraid if you knew about her, you'd—"

"I'd never reject Emma."

"But how could I have known that? My father wasn't nearly the playboy you are—were—and he hated the obligation we forced on him. He hated that my mother and I stripped him of his future. He died a depressed, miserable man because of it. Because of me."

"You ever think it was your father who was at fault for not crafting a better future out of the choice he made?"

"He didn't make the choice," she insisted. "My mother and I foisted it upon him."

"I'm pretty sure *you* had nothing to do with your father's decision to sleep with your mother," he observed dryly.

She bit her lip and cast her gaze toward her shoes. "Even so, I was the unfortunate result."

"Don't say that," he ordered, tipping her face back up. Anger radiated from his expression. "Ever. They were damn lucky to have you."

She hadn't relied on a man to validate her worth for a long,

long time. And having Stephen do so made her feel off balance, as if the bedrock upon which she'd built her life had suddenly turned to quicksand. "I don't want your pity," she said, stepping back to create more space between them. "I only told you this because I wanted you to understand my reluctance to tell you about Emma."

His eyes flashed. "I would never hurt our daughter." He stepped closer, lifting both hands to her shoulders and forcing her to meet his gaze. "No matter what happens, I will never make her feel that I resent her for being born."

She blinked, forcing her voice to remain steady. "Thank you for saying that."

"I didn't just say it. I meant it. Emma's my daughter, Colette. Mine. And I never intentionally wound what's mine."

She remained silent as her throat thickened, the icy barriers she'd nurtured for so long threatening to crack. To thaw.

His grip on her shoulders gentled. Turned into a subtle caress as his thumbs brushed over the knobs of flesh and bone. "Do you believe me?" he asked quietly.

"Yes," she whispered.

"And just because I demanded marriage when I found out about Emma, it doesn't mean we'd be unhappy the way your parents were."

"We would be."

"What makes you so sure?"

"Because you never would have asked to marry me if Emma weren't in the picture."

"How can you possibly know that?"

"Don't you?"

"No." The word held an edge of finality she'd never heard from him before. "Neither of us does. Who's to say what might have happened if you hadn't conceived Emma? Maybe we would have gone together to Paris. Maybe instead of breaking things off with you I'd have decided I couldn't live without you, child or no child."

Confusion rioted in her chest, making it hard to breathe. "But you never—"

"My point is, you don't know what might have developed had you not gotten pregnant. Nobody does. But looking backward instead of forward is getting us nowhere. We have Emma now, and we have to do what's best for our child."

"And you know what's best?"

"I do." His hands drifted up to the sides of her neck to cup her face. "Marry me, Colette."

Her chest heated, dreaded warmth seeping through her limbs and her heart, unveiling the weak vulnerability she'd kept hidden for so long. "But how can a marriage without love be what's best for our child?

"Do you think so little of our ability to make a marriage work without it?"

"How can I not? My father wasn't a bad man. My mother wasn't a bad woman. But they were miserable just the same because the foundation of love wasn't there."

"I would wager their misery had more to do with contempt and blame than with any lack of love."

"Easy for you to say. You weren't there."

He stared at her for several long moments. "Do you respect me?"

Unwilling to lie, she swallowed and quietly admitted, "Yes."

His thumbs grazed the ridge of her jaw, caressing the tip of her chin as he tilted her head back. "Admire me? Enjoy my company? Find me marginally attractive?"

The questions heated her like the kiss of flame, filling her with longing and fear. "You know I do."

The press of his thumbs beneath her chin kept her from avoiding his eyes. "I've known successful marriages built on far less. Haven't you?"

"Yes, but—"

"While at the same time I can point to dozens of marriages

supposedly built on love that deteriorated into horrible, messy, emotional train wrecks within six months." When she might have countered his point, his fingers rose to cover the seam of her lips. "It's respect, trust, and a willingness to compromise that build successful marriages. Not love. And you have to admit that things would be a lot less confusing for Emma if she had only one house, one home, and one unified parental front to contend with."

Deep within, a small voice urged her to accept his logic, to claim whatever tiny piece of his life he was willing to share despite the risk to her wounded heart.

"It'll be better for Emma if we're together," he said softly. "Can't you see that?"

When she still didn't answer, he leaned forward and dipped his head to hers. "Help me make a family for our daughter," he murmured against her mouth. "Marry me."

His lips were firm. Warm. And the tip of his tongue leisurely stroked her lips, as if he had all the time in the world to convince her to change her mind. A shudder of surrender ripped through her, eroding the walls she'd mortared together with hard won independence and salty tears.

"Say yes," he urged.

A tremor started low, gathering speed as it worked its way up between her legs. And because it felt like he was giving her a choice, his proposal drawing heat from her toes to the straining tips of her breasts, her initial resistance wavered.

Could she agree to a marriage without love? Could she overlook the needs of her own damaged heart, her own pitiful, impossible desire to love and be loved, in order to make her child happy? Because, as awful as it was to admit, she knew if she refused him now it wouldn't be because of Emma.

It would be because of her own fear.

She had the dizzying sensation of straddling the shifting fissure of an earthquake, not knowing which side to choose. Suspended in indecision, she withdrew enough to look at

Stephen's intent face, trying to read the future behind features that, until this point, could only be relied on for the here and now. Did she choose the security and safety of being always emotionally alone and separate, or did she choose Stephen and the dual pleasure and pain he was sure to bring?

"We can make it work, I promise," he murmured as his mouth slowly returned to hers.

CHAPTER ELEVEN

WITH her heart thrashing against her ribs and her breath a ragged counterpoint to her pulse, she looped her arms around his neck and returned his kiss in a tentative, nonverbal plea for more time. He remained perfectly still for one protracted second, before reaching for the curve of her hip, his fingers as light as a butterfly's kiss as they settled against her. She knew she could back away, change her mind and break his cautious hold, but something about his uneven breath convinced her to stay.

"Is this your way to avoid giving me an answer?" he breathed, separating just enough to grant her space for second thoughts.

She closed her eyes and nodded.

"Look at me," he said, waiting until she reluctantly complied. "You might distract me with this right now, but I'm not going to stop asking. I want to marry you, Colette."

Biting her lip, she acknowledged his words with a single nod. "I know."

"You don't know how hard these past few weeks have been, pretending that I don't," he said hoarsely. "Being with you and not being able to touch you." His wide palm slid back and around to her buttocks, shaping the soft cotton over the quivering curve. He urged her closer with the slightest hint of pressure, inching her forward until their knees bumped. "It's been hell."

Hypnotized, Colette felt his large hands as he canvassed the landscape of her body: the curved line of her back, the notch of her waist, the swell of hip and thigh, the sensitive inner crook of her elbows and her limp, unprotesting hands.

Her pulse rushed within her ears and she tried to look away from him, to reclaim the emotional space she'd need if she were to survive making love to him again. She failed miserably. She couldn't make her emotions obey, let alone her trembling body. It was if Stephen's piercing blue eyes tethered her to him, building an inescapable heat as his dexterous hands slipped the top few buttons of her shirt free and then returned to cup her now accessible breasts.

The thin barrier of her lace and ribbon bra provided scant protection from the heat of his palms, from the drugging, drifting forays of his thumbs against her hungry flesh. She sucked in an oxygen-starved breath, her thighs trembling and her knees threatening to give way as he lifted the soft weight of her breasts, cupping the pale, lace-encased flesh.

His focus trained on the visible, hardening peaks of her nipples, he leant forward, buffeting the reaching tips with his hot breath. And then he closed that final, torturous distance between them and took her in his mouth.

Heat and moisture filtered through the web of lace, seeping pleasure through to her skin. His tongue stroked, circled, abraded, spearing her with pleasure while excitement gathered. Coiled. Climbed.

"Colette," he whispered, his voice raw and scraping. "You're so beautiful...." He lost a degree of his smooth finesse, his hands fumbling with hurried urgency. Soon her shoulders were bare, the collar of her shirt spread wide enough to anchor her upper arms to her sides.

Beneath the opened blouse, she felt the edge of satin strap and cotton against her upper arms. "Stephen," she said, her fingers plucking helplessly at his ribs. Whimpering, she tried to marshal her own flagging control. "I want..."

But then he released the last of her buttons and tugged her shirt free from the wrapped waistband of her skirt. His head dipped low while his fingers dispensed with her blouse and then returned to the tiny clasp between her breasts. Steadily, insistently, he tugged until satin and lace released its hold on her flesh entirely.

Dropping the combination of fabrics to the floor, he filled his hands with her curves, spreading damp kisses over her sensitized flesh. He caught a reddened nipple between his lips and sucked it deep within his mouth, his splayed hands lifting her bare breasts to his greedy worship. She shuddered, her hands fluttering helplessly at the sides of his cheeks.

"Tell me," he said against her dampened flesh. "Tell me you want this…"

Colette couldn't find the words, couldn't find the thoughts when his lips and tongue and hands splintered her so completely.

Taking her silence as encouragement, Stephen growled in pleasure and lifted her within his arms. A series of steps later, he'd deposited them both on his wide, masculine bed. With his large body canted over hers and one hand cupping her face, Colette might have felt vulnerable. But instead she felt protected and safe. He lowered his head and claimed her lips in a hungry, desperation-flavored kiss, his tongue delving deep as it explored all the hidden coves and hollows of her mouth.

She moaned beneath him and lifted her hands to his wide, hard shoulders. Her fingers clung. Held. Pulled him closer. He hummed his approval, shifting his weight until he rocked atop her, his hips moving in subtle invitation until her thighs fell open to accommodate the press of his pelvis. He released her jaw and his wide hand tracked the contour of her side from rib to waist and thigh. Then his fingers trailed farther, reaching the back of her knee and cocking her leg high.

He lowered his head and pressed his mouth against hers,

while his hand skimmed back up to bracket her jaw within his wide palm. Stephen didn't just kiss her. He devoured her. His mouth demanded while his hand positioned her head for his ravaging. He tasted of barely leashed strength, of desire, and a spicy note of pent-up arousal.

Ripping his mouth aside, Stephen leaned back to look at her, his gaze trailing heat until, in a slow, deliberate motion, his hand found her right breast. Her nipple peaked beneath his touch, a hard knot of pleasure that grew tighter as his fingers closed around it and tugged gently, pulling and pinching until a whimper of pleasure leaked from her throat.

A strained huff of breath hissed between his teeth and he abandoned her breast to lower his hand to the hem of her skirt, before settling his palm against the cluster of curls hidden beneath a prim pair of white panties. She bucked toward his hand, and a low growl of satisfaction rumbled in his chest when he discovered the hint of betraying moisture between her legs. Crushing her mouth in another ferocious kiss, he curled his hand to cup her, his expert fingers delving beneath the cotton underwear.

She gasped and squirmed, the sweet torture of his touch climbing until he parted her flesh and stroked her with a delicate brush of his finger. She shuddered and then froze, every nerve coiling up tight. Her lungs seized, light gathered at the edges of her vision, and if she hadn't already been horizontal she would have crumpled to the mattress with nothing more than a moan. He laughed with a confident huff of sound and simply stroked deeper, spreading her to his expert touch while his mouth ravaged hers.

"I want to kiss you there," he breathed against her lips.

Heat flooded her as a frisson of pleasure rocketed through her womb. She pressed up against him while deep, deep within, she shuddered and trembled and wept. A single fingertip explored her with leisurely, focused intent, mimicking the rhythm of lovemaking while firing her desire for more.

More. He skirted the opening to her body, advancing and retreating, until she bit her lips and chased his hand with small, desperate nudges of her hips. Her body shuddered when his clever fingers skimmed the tiny, tight bud of sensation hidden within. Tremors claimed her limbs and she arched back into the mattress and clung to his shoulders, hanging on tight while an unbearable tension built and built and built.

"Tell me you want this," he rasped, his low voice a hum of demand beneath the roar of her pulse.

"I…"

"Tell me you want more."

He removed his hand and frustrated need clawed through her body.

He held her chin with his long fingers and forced her to look at him. "Tell me."

Desperate now, she nodded within his palm, clinging to him and drawing him close with both hands.

"Yes?" he demanded, his touch still hovering an eternity away.

"Yes!" she gasped, pressing her breasts against his chest and cocking her pelvis toward his elusive hand.

She no longer cared about logic or reason. Everything had vanished beneath the burning need for release. Her second thoughts and caution were as elusive as mist. She didn't care what happened afterward. She didn't care about the future. As long as he didn't stop, she'd give him anything.

A delicious quiver stole over her limbs and contracted within her belly as she felt his fingertip return home and dip a fraction of an inch inside her. *"Yes."*

He withdrew to circle the entrance to her body, and then slid the full length of his finger inside. Each long, deep stroke brought her closer to the brink of rapture. Her head drifted to the side and her eyes closed while a coil of pleasure twisted so tight she thought she'd faint. Or scream. Or maybe even die. Shaking now, she felt a cluster of moans back up in her throat while she struggled for control.

Oh… The one finger turned to two and his thumb resumed its torturous teasing. Circling. Teasing. The delicious dance of his touch against her flesh made sparks ignite behind her eyes. Helpless before him, her hips thrust hungrily toward his hand, drawing him back from each retreat with greedy clamps of her inner muscles.

"Kiss me," she panted, reaching to pull his head down to hers. She needed the taste of him, the pressure of his mouth on hers. "Please…"

He dipped his head, his breath skimming her swollen lips. "Marry me," he told her, denying her.

She tugged on his neck, their mingled breath fracturing the air beneath his hovering mouth. Under her hands his neck was tense, his body taut with banked arousal.

"That's not fair," she panted as she arched up against his hand.

Her lungs seized as she felt his fingers abandon her again. She trembled as he caught both of her hands and pressed them back onto the mattress. Letting go of her entirely.

His blazing eyes demanded more than she'd thought herself capable of giving. "Marry me."

She squeezed her eyes shut while the ache of unfulfilled longing muddled her thoughts. "I can't!"

He shuddered and seemed to have trouble breathing. "I'm sorry to hear that," he said, and he exited the bed and moved toward the door he'd closed behind them.

"Wait!" Abashed, she surged from the bed, before realizing she was still naked above the waist. Embarrassed, and aching with need, she reached to cross her arms over her bare chest. "Don't go."

He turned, and his focus dropped to her canted arms and the pathetic way she tried to protect herself from coming pain. "Then make me stay."

A torrent of second thoughts warred with the desires of her body, tossing her headlong into a sea of indecision and fear. "I'm scared," she whispered.

"I know, sweet. I am too." He said nothing more to convince her, remaining silent and still as he waited for her to make the decision that would direct their future.

And that, more than anything, spurred her into taking the leap. "Ask me again," she whispered.

"Will you be my wife?"

Nervous but resolute, she lowered her arms to her sides, lifted her chin, and then strode to him. When she lifted her palms to the center of his chest, to the space where heat and desire and resolve beat beneath his white shirt, she could feel his apprehension in the rapid thud of his heart. "Yes."

"Yes?" he asked huskily.

"Yes," she repeated in an equally soft voice as she moved her hands to the small white buttons of his shirt and proceeded to slide each one from its hole. "Emma deserves an intact family," she admitted as she dropped her gaze to her splayed fingers. "So, yes, I'll marry you."

"You won't regret it."

"Maybe. Maybe not. But I'm willing to try to anyway," she said.

When she reached the waistband of his denims, she tugged on the ends of his shirt, freeing its bottom edge so she could complete her task. Once she'd released the last button the shirt sagged open, revealing burnished skin and tense muscles that twitched beneath her intent gaze. Colette shoved the rumpled cotton back and slid her hands along his ribs, her thumbs tracking twin ridges of bone in soft, gentle exploration.

His eyes drifted to half-mast and his warm hands rose to cover hers. "Colette. I promise I'll do everything in my power not to hurt you."

Except love me. "I know," she said, shaking off his hands

and then trailing her fingertips up to his sternum, to the springy hair that was scented with the evidence of his earlier arousal.

He inhaled sharply, his hand rising to stall her exploration before she drifted any further. Gripping her wrists, he dipped his head to warn, "We'll be married tomorrow. I won't be put off."

"You never were one to procrastinate."

When he still retained her wrists, his thumbs pressing hard against the rapid pulse beneath her palms, she leaned forward and kissed his bare chest. She brushed her lips over the faint dusting of hair, touching, caressing, urging, until he released her wrists in favor of her head and dragged her up for a lush, voracious kiss. She welcomed the heat of his questing tongue, rejoiced in the avid pressure of his mouth. Her eager fingers, now freed, resumed their hungry exploration. She felt the tiny points of his flat brown nipples, tentatively skimmed her thumbs over both.

He growled, dipped his knees, and lifted her within his arms. She continued kissing him, leaving a damp trail on his cheeks, jaw and throat, until he laid her down on the bed. She reached for his neck, pulling him close and breathing, "Make love to me."

"Wild horses couldn't keep me away." He deposited her on the bed and then straightened just long enough to tug free of his shirt before joining her.

She felt the mattress dip beneath his weight, then turned to welcome him with outstretched arms. He canted up onto one elbow and reached for the side of her face. Dipping his head, he covered her mouth with his, drawing her back into the compelling heat that made her heart thrash within her chest.

She curled toward him, her outside knee drawing up along his outer thigh. She marveled at the differences between before and now. Before she'd loved him they'd made love with wild abandon, two healthy adults in their prime, eager to experiment and explore. Now he touched her with reverence, his fingertips drifting over her skin as if she were a precious work of art too valuable to treat with anything but the utmost care.

It made it easier to pretend he loved her.

Closing her eyes, she surrendered to the sensations he wrought. He drew faint circles down her hip and thigh, slowly working his way down to the sensitive back of her knee. Shifting back onto his own knees, he continued his way south with his mouth, depositing butterfly touches and soft, glancing kisses on her sternum, her ribs, the tender cove of her stomach.

She hummed and arched beneath him, wanting more than just his mouth against her flesh. She wanted the weight of him against her, the hot, slick union of their most intimate flesh. "Hurry," she murmured, reaching for his head.

He smiled up at her with glittering eyes before settling his face against the inner curve of her thigh. He moved his head slowly from side to side, skimming her flesh with an alternating press of lip and whisker. "You always were impatient," he teased, tickling her.

"I just know what I like," she said, flexing her toes as his mouth inched incrementally higher.

"As do I." His hands expertly slid her underwear off her legs and then pressed her knees wide enough that his shoulders fit between them. "I remember everything that pleases you."

He bent over her, his clever fingers opening her before him. She felt the startling slick press of his tongue, its wet, insistent stroke right at the apex of her thighs, and her body jerked in response. She whimpered, a terrified pleasure arrowing through her as he settled heavily over her, pinning her beneath him. He stroked her center again, his sinuous tongue paralyzing all thoughts of protest.

She gasped incoherently and he lifted his head. "You still like this, don't you?" he asked with husky confidence.

She squeezed her eyes shut. "It's been a long time."

"Good." Stephen widened her legs even more, his mouth dragging heat and moisture in its wake while his hands soothed her second thoughts. She felt him everywhere: her ribs, her stomach, her thighs. He exhaled against her intimate flesh, cooling her before he dipped to taste and toy and tease. She surged up against his mouth, lost in a blaze of pleasure so sharp it brought tears to her eyes. All too soon, the steady, constricting circles he drew upon her had her bucking and shaking and pleading aloud for mercy.

And still he plied her flesh, his tongue invading her with devastating softness. The savage sensation of losing control, of quivering atop a chasm of release so acute, had Colette fighting for control at the same time as he urged her surrender. Her heart thrashed within her ribs, she could no longer keep her eyes open, and her knees pulled high as she rocked and rocked and rocked against his mouth. Exquisite pleasure twisted high as he consumed her, until the steady slide of tongue and lip and heat became too much, too intense, too…too *everything*. She catapulted into careening spasms of rapture, contractions cresting in wave after wave as she shuddered and groaned.

After the last ripple of release faded, Stephen raised his head to peer into Colette's flushed face. Her eyes, wet with tears, were too blurred to see clearly. She felt his thumbs wipe the tears from her cheeks and she blinked, reaching to brush her fingers against his mouth. He moved up her body, bracing his weight on his elbows as he settled against her.

She parted for him without hesitation. She knew, down to her last cell, that he wouldn't hurt her. Not now, at least. Not yet. And then he dipped his head to kiss her.

"Help me," he murmured, shifting his weight as they worked to free him from his pants.

She heard the snick of a condom wrapper, watched as he rolled it down his jutting length, and then felt the heavy nudging pressure of his arousal. He rocked gently against her, entering her one slow, exquisite inch at a time until she'd stretched to accommodate his thick length. Adrift in the perfection of their fit, she tipped her pelvis, drawing him even deeper. The angle of penetration sent a new jolt of bliss through her. Eager to grant him the pleasure he'd granted her, she flattened her hands against Stephen's buttocks and then dragged her fingers up the quivering cords of muscle along his spine as she tilted toward him again.

Buried to the hilt within her welcoming heat, Stephen reached for her hips to still their movements. "Just a minute," he said thickly against the scented curve of her neck. "When you move like that, I—"

Lifting her hips, she offered another encouraging nudge as she felt his tension peak.

"Wait!" he gasped. "Colette... I can't..."

She ignored him, pulling as much of his length inside as possible, and the silky slide of her acceptance sent him over the edge. He thrust once, twice, and then climaxed with a groan, her name ripping from his throat.

A long, breathless, shuddering minute later, he lifted his head and scowled at her. "You cheated."

"And you didn't?" she parried, feeling beautifully feminine and powerful beneath the long, lovely weight of his body. She nudged her hips toward his again and an answering tremor of response rippled through them both. "Two can play at this game, you know."

Laughing, he rolled to his back, hauling her with him. He gripped her head and pulled her down, her blond curls making a fragrant curtain around their faces, and kissed her roughly before nipping her lower lip with his teeth. "Minx," he teased.

Three hours later, after he'd taught her all sorts of delightful new variations in the rules of this new game of theirs, she declared a limp surrender. She was nothing but a sated, boneless heap of damp limbs, all hint of reserve and resistance vanquished.

She didn't even think to turn off the lights before she drifted off into a deep, dreamless sleep.

CHAPTER TWELVE

COLETTE awoke when shafts of bright sunlight filtered through her closed eyelids, contrasting with the chill of her exposed shoulders. Disoriented and blinking, she moved to tug the blankets higher. They refused to move. Stuck beneath a decidedly male hip and a long, hairy leg, her paltry efforts to dislodge them accomplished nothing. Instantly awareness flooded her, along with the realization that she was as naked as a newborn babe. She lifted an arm to cover her breasts, rosy and warm despite the chill. A broad, browned hand stilled the motion.

"Don't," came Stephen's sleep-roughened voice. "I want to see your skin in the sunlight."

He was awake. Watching her. Warmth radiated from her stomach, turning the tips of her exposed breast to a hard, knotted pink.

"Lovely," he breathed, the back of his hand rising to brush delicately against her nipple. "You look good enough to eat, do you know that?"

In the light of dawn, her impulsive decision of the night before rushed back with bruising, jarring clarity. What had she been thinking? She'd made love to him. She'd agreed to marry him. And now her heart was so full of longing and love she didn't know how to contain it all. How would she ever survive once he realized he no longer wanted her? How

could she ever live as his wife in name only, pretending she
was happy so that their child didn't feel insecure?

"Hey," he said, jostling her out of her morose thoughts.
"Why the long face?"

Rather than reply, she leaned toward him, pressing her
mouth to his. It was easier than talking.

He obliged her with a deep kiss that sent her pulse careening yet again. Sliding her over the sex-scented sheets,
he tucked her up against his flesh, his warm, wide palms
cupping her buttocks as he pulled her in close. It was easy to
feel safe when they were kissing, when she could bury her
second thoughts behind the blurring effect of desire. So she
reached for the rigid length of his erection where it strained
against her stomach, circling his thick circumference and
slowly sliding south. Then north. Then south again.

"Do you have another condom?" she breathed against his
lips.

He obliged her with startling swiftness, and this time she
was the one to slide it down his eager length. She took her
time, concentrating on the here and now and steeping herself
in the heady power she wielded over him. He held himself
still, watching her through slitted eyes, until she pressed her
thumb against the broad tip and gently squeezed. He jerked
within her hand with a groan, and then pulled her up for a
wild, voracious kiss.

Scant seconds later he twisted to his back, with her atop
him, and pressed her onto his length in one long, smooth,
sleek slide. She gasped in surprise, the ease with which he'd
impaled her sending shudders of delight clear to her scalp.

"We still fit perfectly, don't we?" he said, his eyes glittering from beneath a fan of black lashes.

Physically, yes. But in all the ways that mattered...?

Don't think about it. Determined to wring as much pleasure
from this idyllic interlude as she could before reality intervened, she flung her head back and closed her eyes. Setting

a steady rhythm, she angled her hips so he stroked her with every pass. She lifted, pressed, tilted, the pace of their love-making slowly increasing as her pleasure spiraled, spread, and climbed to an almost unbearable peak. Having him inside her like this was so...so...

Thoughts failed her as she reached the summit, her body trembling and spasming with each delicious stroke. An aching combination of desperation and love filled her heart to brimming as Stephen gripped her hips, drawing out the pulsing pleasure of her inner muscles. Clenching him deep inside, she leaned to balance against the granite plane of his stomach while he found his own bucking release. Watching the play of emotions in his face, knowing that she'd brought him the same intense pleasure he'd brought her, made her want to weep.

If only it could always stay like this. If only she could meet all his needs with the same degree of success. If only she could claim his heart as easily as she claimed his body.

Afterward, she remained draped over his damp chest, toying idly with the black fleece beneath her hand. She stroked his skin, relearning the contours of his ribs, the transition of muscle to bone to muscle again at his side. She might have slept for a while. Might even have dreamed a bit.

Much, much later, he awakened her with a soft murmur against her rumpled hair.

"Hey, sweet, it's time."

Disoriented, she blinked, sitting up to rub her eyes. He looked freshly shaved, showered, and ready for the day. "Time? For what?"

His blue eyes flashed with fiery heat while his mouth curved in a seductive, triumphant smile. "To get married, of course. The justice of the peace arrives in less than an hour."

"An hour?" she squeaked.

"You did agree to today, didn't you?" he asked in a mild voice.

She had. But somehow, in the light of day, she couldn't remember why. Terrified, backed into a corner and mute, she simply stared at him, her retraction filling her throat.

"I've called the hotel spa and they're sending over their top two stylists." He checked his watch. "They should be here in about five minutes to help you get ready."

"Get ready?" Horrified that tears were beginning to sting the back of her nose, she blinked away her girlish dreams for a romantic wedding and swallowed. Hard. "But I don't even have a dress."

"Yes, you do," he said, a hint of satisfaction coloring his tone as he gestured toward a garment bag hanging on his corner coat rack. "I took the liberty of choosing a wedding dress for you the day I found out about Emma. The saleswoman assured me it would fit."

"The day you...?" she repeated through quivering lips. "Why would you do such a thing?"

"I didn't want you to look back on this day with regrets."

As if she'd have anything *but* regrets.

"This is for you as well." He reached in his suit jacket pocket and withdrew a small blue box, wrapped in its signature Tiffany ribbon.

"You don't have to give me a ring," she told him, avoiding his extended hand.

"This is not about what I have to do," he said, lifting her rigid fingers and pressing the box into her palm. "It's about what I want to do. For you."

She bit her lip and ducked her head, reluctantly removing the ribbon and lifting the hinged velvet top. The morning light slanted across a giant solitaire diamond, bigger than the lump in her throat. The engagement ring glittered brightly, a stark contrast to the aching despair filling her heart.

"It's too much," she protested, closing the lid and extending the box back toward him. "I can't wear this."

"Put it on," he told her.

"But it's a ring for someone who—"

"Now."

She obeyed in silence, her lungs tight. Seeing the weighty ring on her finger, knowing that he'd chosen it as a mark of ownership over her, she felt the tension in her chest increase even more.

You can do this. For Emma, you can do this.

Less than forty-five minutes later, after a hurried makeup treatment and style, Colette looked every inch the flushed, nervous bride. The stylists had coiled her hair into an ornate, pearl-encrusted upsweep that exposed her neck and left wispy strands of blond trailing along one cheek and her nape. Her dress—a gorgeous beaded silk sheath—cinched in at the waist, boned through the bodice, and ending two inches above her knees—made the most of her modest curves and exposed far too much of her chest and arms. Her new three-inch heels, a concession to femininity she rarely allowed herself, made her legs look like they went on forever.

Looking at herself in the mirror, she realized she'd never looked so beautiful. She bit her shiny coral lips, feeling like an utter fraud. What madness had she agreed to?

By the time she walked to Stephen's elegant study and stood next to him before an elderly, rheumy-eyed justice of the peace, she felt trapped in a nightmare from which there was no escape. The panic Colette had been fighting for the past hour knotted in her chest, her breath so rapid and shallow it felt like she was hyperventilating.

Dizzy, her legs weak, and her hands clenching the small bouquet of flowers Stephen had gathered from his garden, she forced herself to remain at Stephen's side without collapsing. Trembling, she locked her knees and faced the officiant.

Without shifting his focus from the justice of the peace, Stephen reached to collect her hand, aligning his warm, dry palm against hers. Stephen's secretary and Janet, along with a beaming Emma garbed in smocked white batiste, served as the only witnesses to their union.

"We are gathered here to celebrate the union of Stephen Whitfield and Colette Huntington," the officiant intoned as he surveyed their tiny group of five over a pair of wire-rimmed spectacles. "We honor their commitment to each other, and to the future they will create together…"

As the ceremony continued, Colette was excruciatingly aware of Stephen's fingers threaded between hers. He stood as still as stone, his profile serious and his posture erect. When it came time to exchange their vows, Stephen reached to collect her bouquet and then handed it to his secretary. Turning back to her, he claimed both her empty hands with his.

His blue eyes focused on her face, refusing to release her gaze, while he professed his intentions for their future life together. "I, Stephen, take you, Colette, to be my wife. I promise above all else to be honest and faithful, and to honor you as my partner and spouse. I promise to raise our children with love and devotion and to do my best to foster joy and peace in our home. I give you my hand, my support, my trust and my name as I join my life to yours."

The knot in her throat turned into a boulder, and suddenly she couldn't see through the tears misting her eyes. "I, Colette, take you Stephen, to be my husband…" Her voice shook, but she cleared her throat and made it to the end without falling apart.

And then it was time for them to exchange rings. Goosebumps rode her flesh as he slid a platinum band on her icy finger. His eyes remained on hers, steady and calm and somehow comforting, despite the surreal circumstances of their union.

"Just as this circle has no end, my commitment to you is eternal," he promised, without a trace of unsteadiness in his voice. "With this ring, I take you to be my partner for life."

Her gooseflesh grew into an uncontrollable trembling by

the time she reached for his hand and pushed a matching ring down his long, tanned finger. The ring caught on his knuckle and a small smile lifted one corner of his mouth. He reached to help, and then bolstered her with both hands. She blinked, inhaled sharply, and whispered her commitment to the only man with the power to destroy her.

"…I now pronounce you man and wife," concluded the magistrate. "You may kiss the bride."

Stephen gently drew her close against his body and bent his head to hers. For a moment their breath mingled. And then his lips touched hers in a sweet, supple kiss that carried more promise than heat. Dizzy, she swayed against him, and his broad hands slid up to her shoulders to anchor her. Feeling his smile beneath her lips, and suddenly aware of their audience, she flushed when he eased away from her with a gentle push against her upper arms.

A flurry of congratulations later, the papers had been signed, the justice of the peace had been dispatched, and the small wedding party stood in a loose circle, grinning at each other. All except Colette, that was. She felt like she'd been caught in a hurricane: buffeted by winds too fierce to fight, disoriented, and unable to manage anything more complicated than simple breathing.

"You made a beautiful bride, dear," said Janet, reaching to brush a stray curl from Colette's cheek. "And Mr. Whitfield made a very handsome groom."

"And Stephen here, despite his wild ways, is a good boy," said Stephen's secretary as she squeezed Colette's bare shoulder. "Treat him well and he'll make you a fine husband."

"Of course I will," said Stephen, reaching to haul her back to his side. "Stop scaring her."

The two witnesses exchanged an amused glance and then laughed. "All new brides are scared," said Janet. "It's your job to set her fears to rest."

Her husband—her *husband*!—grinned and then wrapped

a possessive arm about her waist. "I fully intend to do so," he said with a grin toward both matronly women. She sensed a shift in his purpose as he turned to query his secretary, "Is everything arranged?"

She bobbed her head and then dug in her wide bag for a travel binder. Extending it to Stephen, she said, "The tickets are inside, along with contact numbers for all involved parties."

"Tickets?" Colette asked. "What tickets?"

"Janet?" he said, ignoring Colette. "Are our bags packed?"

"Yes, sir, they are." Her face pleated in a wide smile. "I even threw in a few extra things I thought you might need."

"Excellent. Why don't you and Emma go fetch them while Colette and I have a few moments to talk?"

The two giddy females tripped out of the room with Emma in tow, obviously relishing their role as coconspirators in Stephen's plans to kidnap his new wife.

"Stephen," Colette said, turning to face her new husband with alarm tightening her belly. "What is going on?"

Stephen hauled her back into his arms, anchoring his groin against hers and leaning to breathe against her neck. "I'm taking you on a honeymoon."

"Honeymoon!" she blurted as she arched back within his arms. The prospect of spending days alone with him in a romantic setting while trying to maintain her emotional distance sent terror winging through her veins. "But we can't leave Emma!"

"We're not. I've arranged for Janet and Emma to accompany us."

Colette's thoughts churned, trying to adjust to this unexpected turn of events. "But what about the Renaissance? Isn't its grand reopening in three weeks?"

He cocked a brow. "Everything is right on schedule, and I'll just be a phone call away if anything goes wrong." He stared down at her, obviously bemused by her panicked attempts to delay. "Why do I get the impression you don't want to take a honeymoon with me?"

She pressed against his chest with both splayed hands, unable to think properly with him so close. "One bed's as good as another, don't you think? We don't really have to go anywhere exotic to have sex."

His eyes narrowed as he studied her face. "Is what you think this is about? Sex?"

The low note of warning in his voice cinched her trepidation into worry. "Isn't it?"

His grip against her waist tightened. "No, Colette. It's about building a marriage. About a husband wanting to please his new wife."

She shook her head while her stomach trembled in protest. "But honeymoons are for couples who love each other." She blinked, refusing to allow the emotions that hovered treacherously close to the surface to show. "And we don't, remember?"

"I want this to be a new start for us, Colette." He lifted a hand to cup her jaw while probing her gaze with his. "So why don't we just see how it plays out?"

CHAPTER THIRTEEN

"Do you want to eat our luncheon out here or inside?" Stephen asked several afternoons later, as he approached her lounger on their private seafront patio.

She squinted up at him from beneath her wide-brimmed hat, his gorgeous body outlined by the Mediterranean sun and the blue, blue sky of the French Riviera.

He handed her a glass of sparkling water and smiled. "The butler has brought our meal and wants to know where to set it up."

"Wherever you want it is fine," she said, fighting the flush of warmth seeing him brought to her chest. "Will Emma and Janet be joining us?"

"No. Emma fell asleep and Janet said she'd wait for her to wake up." He'd slung a white beachtowel over his bare shoulders, and the contrast between the bleached terrycloth and his bronzed skin made Colette's mouth water.

Despite all the times they'd made love…she'd lost count a few days back…she still wanted him as much as she had the first time. He could set her aflame with nothing more than a look. And the look he was sending her now made her grateful for the chilled water between her palms.

"I think Emma's morning in the sun exhausted her," he continued, his smile telling her full well that he'd read her mind.

He's talking about our daughter. And all you're thinking about is sex.

"She claimed France has the best sand ever," Colette said, averting her eyes and sucking in a steadying inhale. "We spent the morning slathered in sunblock and building castles fit for even the finest of princesses. You'd have been quite impressed with her budding architectural skill."

"I'm sorry I missed it."

"Me too." It was the truth. She missed him in the mornings, while he dealt with his European business concerns and traded terse phone calls with Whitfield relatives. "Did you finish what you needed to do today?"

"Most of it. But we'll need to detour to London on our way home. There are some issues at the Grand that require my personal attention."

"Anything serious?"

His jaw flexed for a faint beat of time before his mouth stretched into a smile. A smile that didn't quite reach his eyes. "Nothing you need to worry your beautiful head over."

He was hiding something from her. Something that had to do with the Whitfield family and was pulling his attention from their idyllic honeymoon in ways she shouldn't resent, but did. "Are you sure?"

His gaze dipped from her face to her body, trailing from neck to toe and back again. "You know, I think I'd prefer to eat on the patio," he said without answering her question. "The view out here is gorgeous."

She flushed, exquisitely aware of how much flesh her orange and pink bikini exposed to his view. But she wouldn't allow the heat in his eyes to distract her. "You've spent a lot of time the past few days on the phone with various Whitfields," she insisted. "Are they upset about your marriage to me? Are they angry about Emma?"

"The butler's waiting for his instructions," he said. "And we don't want our luncheon spoiled, do we?" With that, he strode back to the villa, ostensibly to inform the butler as to their plans.

While she waited for him to return, Colette stared out at the glittering Mediterranean water lapping at the shore a mere stone's throw away. As beautifully decadent as it was, the luxury of the hotel's five-star service was becoming more and more difficult to enjoy. White sand, azure water and the soothing rhythm of the sea should have kept her in a blissful state of relaxation. But with each passing day new tentacles of worry twined their way between the roots of her fragile hope.

She could sense Stephen's mounting stress, and beneath the stress she knew resentment crouched in the wings. It was only a matter of time before he accepted that marriage to her, a marriage devoid of love, was too much work. It was only a matter of time before he realized being her husband was an obligation he no longer wished to fulfill.

To distract herself from the morose thoughts that threatened to ruin her mood, she sat up and dug through the giant beachbag she'd packed for the day. There'd be time enough for second thoughts and worries once they returned home. For now, she'd live in the moment. She'd smear herself in another layer of sunscreen and pretend that everything was exactly the way she wanted it to be.

"Need some help?" Stephen's silky voice and the glancing touch of his long hand on her shoulder caught her unawares, sending heat streaking over her skin. The butler had followed Stephen with the same soundless approach, and he discreetly set their table a couple of yards away, his back to the two of them.

Determined to glean as much enjoyment from her time with Stephen as possible, she extended the sunblock and then leaned forward to grant him access to her bare shoulders and back. "Would you?"

She submitted to his careful ministration until the butler left them to their privacy. Her breath hitched when Stephen finished her back and then circled her lounger, beckoning for her to sit back against its striped cushion so he could apply lotion to her chest and throat.

"I can do the rest," she protested.

"I know you can," he said with a smile, his blue eyes crinkling as he nudged the sunblock out of her reach and then held up his glistening fingers. "But I was here first."

Dressed in a pair of blue and white swimming trunks, he looked like an Irish angel gone bad. The long, powerful sweep of his biceps, broad shoulders, and the stretch of tight, rippled muscles over his abdomen drew her gaze and sent a sharp jolt of love spiking through her heart. "Heaven forbid I bump you out of your spot in the queue," she said. Only a slight tremble in her voice betrayed her.

He heard it and, misinterpreting its cause, smiled wickedly. "I knew you'd see reason." His strong hands resumed their lovely massage of her skin, rubbing sunblock into hidden areas that had never even felt the kiss of the sun.

"You move those fingers any lower and I'm going to forget all about sunbathing," she murmured in a breathless attempt to keep things light. Superficial and safe.

His unrepentant grin deepened, though his fingers abandoned her breasts to make a warm sweep down her shoulders and arms. "Am I supposed to think that's a bad thing?"

Her eyes drifted to half mast as his strong hands seduced her away from worries about the future. "I can't decide," she hummed. "You did promise me some food."

A small huff of laughter filled the air between them. "I'll give you a respite," he teased. "For now. At least until we're done eating."

She lolled her head to the side to find him staring at her with amusement in his eyes.

"Or we could postpone lunch?" he asked hopefully.

Smiling, she stared back into his beautiful face. "Not a chance. I'm starving."

"Can't blame a man for trying," he teased as he shifted

his attention to the task at hand, his broad palms spreading warmed lotion down her thighs and over her knees. "I'm coming off of a five-year drought and need to make up for lost time."

Suspecting he lied simply to flatter her, she slanted him a look from beneath the brim of her hat. "A five-year drought? You?"

"Oh, I did my best to bury your rejection of me in the arms of faceless women, but it wasn't nearly as satisfying as I'd hoped." His eyes remained trained on his hands, his tone as light and teasing as before. "I'm afraid you've ruined me for all other women, sweet."

A sudden swell of emotion pitched in her stomach. Though she knew Stephen didn't love her, the thought that he might have missed her as much as she'd missed him filled her with a queer, unnerving dizziness. She had no doubt that he'd try to make their marriage work for Emma's benefit, but it had never occurred to her that he might want to make it work for *her* benefit as well.

When his hands stilled and he lifted his eyes to hers, she realized she'd waited too long to respond. Flustered, she grappled to regain her equilibrium as her cheeks heated with embarrassment.

"You don't believe me, do you?" he asked, his warm gaze gauging her reaction.

"I—I don't even compare to those other women and you know it," she stammered. "They're beautiful, they're wealthy, and they are far more suitable for your world than I could ever hope to be."

"*You're* beautiful. And, trust me, I'd rather have you in my bed than any one of those rich, spoiled socialites."

She blinked, grateful for the shading brim of her hat. "You don't have to fake it for my benefit," she said, pushing the words past her dry throat. "You don't have to pretend I'm the wife you would have chosen had you been given the choice."

"I did have a choice. And I chose you."

"Yes, but…" she started to say. "You only chose me because—"

"I chose you because I wanted *you*," he said flatly. "Providing a good mother for my daughter factored into it, yes, but I'd have wanted you whether we had Emma or not."

"Why? Why would you want me when you don't even love me?" she asked, hating herself for asking but unable to stop the words from tumbling from her mouth.

"Didn't we already discuss this?" He pushed upright and exhaled noisily. "Love destroys people, Colette. It makes them vulnerable and weak and rash. I want no part of it."

"You didn't answer my question."

"I did. You just refuse to hear my answer. I want you for you, Colette. I want you because you're smart. You work hard. You're tough. You're beautiful. You make me laugh and you make me feel like a better person than I am. And, yes, you're an incredible lover and an amazing mother to our child. Can't that be enough?"

No.

"I thought you were hungry," he said, abandoning her and heading toward the table. "And our lunch is getting cold."

Three days later, a gentle breeze rode the Mediterranean air, bringing the scent of the sea and lending a welcome coolness to the evening. But Stephen had difficulty appreciating the temperature or the view. As beautiful as the setting was, he couldn't enjoy it, and it made frustrated anger percolate low in his gut. He felt a pathetic affinity with the sea, sucked by a relentless tide toward a shore he'd been avoiding his whole life.

What was it about women and their irrational need for love? He'd thought Colette was different, that she'd understand and respect his desire to keep love out of the mix. She belonged to him, he belonged to her, and they'd created a beautiful, amazing daughter together. They pleasured each other's bodies, laughed together and respected each other. Why couldn't she just accept it as enough?

The answer beat within his chest like a death knell.

Because, you foolish sot, she wants a relationship built on love.

Love he was incapable of giving her.

And the hell of it was he felt a futile, hopeless urge to try anyway. Catapulted back into the wretched insecurity of his youth, he knew that, no matter how hard he tried, he'd never measure up. The truth ate at him like a cancer. He would never be enough for Colette. He knew it. He was *inadequate* in some essential way, and it was only a matter of time before Colette figured it out and left him.

And, even though she hadn't brought up the topic of love again, things hadn't returned to normal. She still joined him in his bed as often as he wished, but her walls seemed to have grown thicker. If he didn't instigate a conversation she was silent as a tomb. She still smiled when he said amusing things, she never denied him her company when he wanted it, and she shared their daughter and her care without reservation. But he could sense her rising discontent. She wasn't happy, and knowing that she never could be in a marriage with him made him angry, panicked and afraid.

He didn't like the feeling at all.

Irritated, he felt desperation eat away at his gut and simmer in his veins. It wasn't fair. It made him want to yell or fight or hurl curses at the sky.

He didn't, of course. To do so would have been too much like his father, a ruined wreck of a man who hadn't been able to function without his wife. So instead Stephen stuffed the anger down deep and remained alone at the small, linen-draped table long after their butler had cleared away their final honeymoon supper.

As far as meals had gone, it had been their most uncomfortable yet. They'd picked at their food in silence, barely looking at each other and ignoring the undercurrents of tension that seemed to mount with each passing day. When Colette had finished and gone in to bathe Emma and tuck her into bed, Stephen hadn't followed.

An hour later he heard Colette's soft gasp behind him as she exited the bathroom after her shower. He'd moved to their suite's wide, wingback chair, the television remote in his hand and the volume set to low. He knew without turning that she hadn't expected him to be there, and he knew with the same degree of certainty that if he didn't tell her to stay she'd find some excuse to leave him alone in their room.

He waited until he heard the telltale click of the door latch signaling her retreat before he cursed beneath his breath and twisted to catch her before she escaped. "Colette?" he called.

She froze with the door halfway open and then slowly turned to face him, her eyes avoiding his and a pretty blush rising to stain her freckled chest. Scrubbed clean, her skin pink from her shower and her damp hair curling around her neck and darkening the shoulders of her green silk robe, she looked good enough to eat. Except he wanted more than just sex. He wanted her soft and open and happy. With him.

"Yes?" she asked, her narrow hand still gripping the crystal handle of the door.

"Where are you going?"

A silent swallow moved in the long column of her slender neck, and he could see the nervous beat of her pulse beneath her skin. "I thought I'd check on Emma."

"She never wakes up once she goes to sleep. You know that."

She hesitated, just a fraction of a second, and he watched as her posture stiffened. It felt as if she were girding herself for battle, a battle he'd never wanted to fight in the first place.

"I'm not going to bite you," he said, irritation riding his tone.

She hid her hazel eyes behind a fan of brown lashes. "Did I say you were?"

"You act like I am, and I'm tired of always feeling like I have to prove myself to you."

"You don't," she whispered, her lush mouth trembling. "I know who you are and I'm content with that."

"Really? You're content? You're happy?" he said softly, anger and frustration clawing at his chest. "Because it sure as hell doesn't feel like you are."

Pale as parchment, she said nothing to refute him.

"I didn't think so," he said.

"What do you want from me?"

"I want you to be happy with what we have instead of asking for more."

"I'm trying."

"Are you?"

Her throat moved and her gaze darted to the side. "Yes. I thought I could do this. I *wanted* to. For Emma. But it's too hard."

"*This?* What exactly is *this*?" His tone was sharper than he'd intended and she flinched.

Pressed against the door, she looked ready to bolt. He knew if he reached for her, if he moved toward her at all, she'd be gone. So he forced himself to wait.

"I think we made a mistake," she finally said in a low voice. "It's not working."

"Too bad. Leaving me is not an option."

Her eyes widened with her distress. "What?"

"You don't get to run away this time. Our daughter needs both of us, so even if it's hard, you're not leaving."

"I'd never leave Emma!"

"Neither would I. So I guess we're at an impasse, aren't we?"

"But I can't do this! I can't live this way!"

"You can't live being pampered and adored by a husband who's trying like hell to make his wife happy?"

"But you aren't! Spending money on me and carting me around the world and pleasuring my body won't make me happy."

"Then what will?"

"A real marriage built on love. I want that. I want a family that loves each other, that shares things even when it hurts. I want what you aren't willing to give me."

"Why?"

"Because! This isn't a marriage, Stephen, and I can't keep pretending that it is. I can't live as someone else's obligation."

"Damn it, Colette, this has *nothing* to do with obligation!"

"Then what is it about, huh? Because it sure isn't about love. It's not about closeness or emotional connection."

"I told you. It's about respect. And admiration. And shared goals. It's about a marriage that will make Emma feel secure."

"But you don't respect me. How could you, when I settle for so little? You don't love me and you never will. Whether you admit it or not, I know I trapped you into a marriage you never wanted in the first place, and I can't keep pretending that I'm okay with it."

"You didn't trap me. I trapped you, remember?"

She shook her head, her eyes wide and haunted. "I can't be anybody's burden again, Stephen. I won't."

"You're not a burden."

"Yes. I am." Hiking her trembling chin, she kept her gaze steady despite its sheen of tears. "You don't want a real wife. You don't want a real marriage. And you certainly don't want me."

"Right," he said, his inability to make her see reason churning in his gut. "I don't want you because every man in the world is your father. Because no one could possibly want you when he didn't."

The blood drained from her face at that, casting her

freckles in sharp relief. "This has nothing to do with my father."

"It has *everything* to do with your father, and you're too stubborn to see it." He raked his hands through his hair, frustration and anger coiling through him. "You're stuck in that same hurting, scared place you were in when you were eight years old and you want me to give you the reassurance and love that he never did. But I'm not your father, Colette. I can't make up for what he did to you."

"I never asked you to," she whispered.

"You did. You want love. Love that I can't give you. And I'm sorry if that hurts your feelings, and I'm sorry if that makes you feel like an obligation or a burden when you aren't. I *want* to be married to you. I *want* to build a life with you and raise Emma together. I want things to be easy and happy and uncomplicated. Don't you?"

She stared at him, her mouth quivering and her luminous eyes filling with tears.

"I'm not your father, Colette," he said quietly. "Stop treating me like I am."

A solitary tear trembled and then fell, tracking a silvery trail down her cheek.

He cupped her nape and leaned to stare into her eyes. "I want you to trust me not to hurt you. Even if I don't love you, I'll never hurt you. I promise."

"But you already are," she whispered, moving away from his touch and bracing her shoulders as she lifted her chin. "And the worst part is, you can't even see it."

Clenching his fists, he turned away from her, his chest feeling heavy and tight. "It's obvious we can't discuss this now. Come. I'm tired and I want to go to bed. We can talk about this later."

CHAPTER FOURTEEN

COLETTE stared at his retreating back, wanting to follow him, to explain, to beg him to hold her and soothe away her fears. But how could he when he didn't love her? When he never would?

She blinked, silently holding back the sobs crowding her chest as she watched him shuck his clothing, lift the sheets, and then climb into bed without looking at her. She followed him across the room, removed her robe, and slid in next to him.

For the first time since coming to the Riviera he turned away from her, presenting his broad back. He didn't touch her. He didn't make love to her or wrap his big, warm body around hers.

And she felt the distance between them like a jagged tear in her heart. She wanted to curl into him, to bury her face against his skin and confess her love for him. She wanted him to wind his strong arms around her, to kiss her, reassure her, and tell her again that he'd never regret marrying her. But what would be the use? They were just empty words, meaningless words he'd feel obligated to say.

Somehow Colette managed to keep the sobs buried deep, deep inside. Tears seeped silently from the corners of her eyes, down her temples and onto the pillow, but she didn't make a sound. She didn't move.

She didn't sleep much that night, and their flight to London the next day was tense. Emma distracted her and gave her day purpose. For Emma, she'd feign good spirits. For Emma, she'd pretend everything was fine.

The next night was a repeat of the night before. Just the setting had changed. Though they stayed in the Whitfield Grand's penthouse suite, the same suite she and Stephen had once used for their clandestine lunchtime trysts, it felt as if they were visitors to a museum. Pleasant, cordial and polite, she and Stephen spoke only when conditions demanded it.

And still he didn't touch her.

The following morning, she found a note from him stuck to the bathroom mirror.

Don't wait up tonight; I'll be home late.—S

A call to the front desk informed Colette as to *why* Stephen would be home late. Just like every year since its opening, the Whitfield Grand was hosting the Sir Walter Whitfield III's annual birthday bash. It was scheduled for eight p.m. in the largest ballroom, and everybody who was anybody would be in attendance. While she, Stephen's *wife*, the woman he'd instructed not to *wait up*, hadn't even been invited.

An unexpected flash of anger heated her chest. As irrational as it was, she felt betrayed. True, she wasn't the wife he wanted, and she'd brought a child into the world he'd never intended to have. But for him to keep her from meeting his family, hated or not, spoke volumes about how he really felt about her. The whole time he'd been asking for her trust, claiming to want her for *her*, he'd been lying to her.

He, who'd claimed to want a marriage built on mutual respect, was too embarrassed even to introduce her to his family.

If he'd been honest, if he'd said he married her because she was Emma's mother and she was great in bed, they'd at least have had realistic expectations of each other. She'd have been able to trust him.

But, no. He claimed to want her *happy*. He claimed he'd married her for *her*. Right.

He wanted her so much he'd rather hide her away in a hotel suite than publicly claim her as his wife.

Fine. If that was the way he wanted to play it, she'd play. She'd prove him to be the liar he was and then their marriage could finally be based on truth.

Stephen arrived late to his grandfather's party.

Dressed in the requisite tuxedo, he made a beeline for the bar and ordered a Scotch on the rocks. He didn't want to see his family, didn't want to see any of the spoiled blond Whitfields who'd made his life a living hell. He'd only come out of loyalty to his mother's memory, to remind every damn one of them that he hadn't forgotten what they'd done.

After spending twenty-five years proving that the Whitfields couldn't bully him the way they'd bullied his mother, he wasn't about to stop now. And, Lord knew, if he failed to make an appearance, his spiteful cousins would trash the hotel in the name of victorious celebration.

Just like every other year, the event was packed with people Stephen could barely tolerate when his mood was generous. Europe's richest businessmen, their superficial wives and catty mistresses, celebrities whose names he could never remember, and anyone else fortunate enough to claim a coveted connection to the Whitfields was in attendance. It was enough to sour any mood, and his wasn't good to begin with.

After not touching Colette for days, he felt like a caged tiger spoiling for a kill. Preferably something flavored with a Whitfield sneer and polished platinum hair.

His hand tightened around the tumbler of ice and liquor as his least favorite Whitfield cousin approached him. "Still drinking like the Irish scum that spawned you, eh?"

"What do you want, Liam?"

"Besides everything you took that should have been mine?" he said with a scowl. "I'd be happy if you just disappeared."

"Much as I'd like to help you out, I can't," he said, before slugging back his drink in a single swallow. The burn felt good and the tumbler kept his hands busy. For now. "Who else would clean up after your mistakes if I were gone?"

Liam's eyes narrowed and a telltale flush of fury stained his face a mottled red. "Everything was fine until you showed up, uninvited and unannounced."

"I returned to keep you from driving the Grand into bankruptcy." He kept his voice calm, though it required a supreme effort to keep his hands off the pompous bastard's neck. "Irritating you is just an unexpected perk."

"You're not good enough to step foot in the Grand, let alone run it. You're the son of a whore, always sniffing around whores." His face screwed into an ugly combination of disgust and jealousy. "You can't even keep them away for Grandfather's birthday, can you?"

"What are you talking about?"

"I'm talking about Colette Huntington, that nobody who acts like she belongs here."

Stephen's gut cinched with a sick lurch. Panic coiled in his lungs, froze the air in his chest. For a black, eternal moment his heart forgot how to beat. Then it surged back to life, thundering hard beneath his ribs, and he spun to locate Colette's golden hair amid the knot of glittering party goers.

No.

He shoved the birthday guests aside without regard for their gasped outrage, leaving offended gossip in his wake as he raced toward his wife. His vulnerable, exposed wife. For a moment he lost sight of her. The ballroom was so crowded he felt as if he navigated a tumultuous sea of jewel and silk. He plunged deeper into the mass of tuxedos and ballgowns until he caught sight of her willowy neck and golden shoulders. It seemed a century since he'd drawn breath, an eon since he'd seen her safe.

Then he saw her companion.

They stood with their backs to him, his grandfather's gnarled hand clutched just above Colette's elbow as they made their way to the edge of the ballroom. Stephen lurched forward, the leaden weight of anxiety twisting within his stomach and making his legs unsteady and weak.

"Colette!"

They turned as one, his wife and his grandfather, and Stephen felt his vision go black on the edges. What had Grandfather said to her? What damage had he already done?

Regal, serene, and utterly composed, Colette didn't show any evidence of his family's attack, but he knew she wouldn't give them the satisfaction. She was strong that way, keeping her pain locked firmly away where no one could see. Except he knew her scars ran deep. He knew her generous, wounded soul couldn't survive the blows his family would deliver.

If only he could breathe, he'd take her away from this place. He'd keep her safe.

"Stephen," she said, arching a prim brow. "Imagine running into you here."

He ignored his grandfather and stared at his wife silently, his thoughts heaving as ineffectively as his chest.

"Your grandfather was just telling me what a terror you were as a child." She smiled down at the old goat, a luminous goddess draped in gold and green. "Weren't you, sir?"

His grandfather glared at Stephen, his icy blue gaze communicating his disapproval as eloquently as any words. "Why didn't you tell us you'd married this *delightful* girl?"

The sarcastic edge beneath his grandfather's words made Stephen's chest cinch more tightly. Did Colette hear it? Did she hear the signature Whitfield disdain beneath the saccharine sentiment? The hint of battle lines being drawn?

Stepping away from his grandfather, she approached him

with a strained smile curving her lips. "Yes, *dear*, why didn't you tell your family we were married?"

He watched her mouth move, but for some reason he couldn't process her words. He couldn't hear above the thundering roar of his pulse. But he could see the muted evidence of her hurt within her hazel eyes. He could see the sheen of tears welling deep behind her wall of unaffected detachment.

"Colette tells us you have a daughter," said the old man in a dangerous, threatening voice. "A lovely little child named Emma. Did you intend to keep *her* from us as well?"

Yes, you sick bastard. I did.

Behind them, the Whitfield vultures circled, his uncles and cousins and their wives inching closer, with malice in their expressions and venom on their tongues. They'd waged their social war for decades and honed their weapons to a sharp, cruel edge. They would cut Colette to ribbons and she didn't even realize the danger.

Somewhere low in his gut, beneath the resting place of all his childhood fears, panic began to build. He'd been here before. He'd seen the terrible effects of the Whitfield poison on innocent women. He'd seen the havoc his family wreaked. *Get her out of here*, a voice in his head clamored. *Now*.

He reached for Colette at the same time his most vitriolic cousin did.

"Colette," Stephen said, pulling her forward, away from his descending family. "Come. We're leaving."

She pulled her arm from his hand, her pleasant party façade immediately overtaken by fury. "Thank you, but, no. I'm having a lovely time."

"Trust me," he warned, reclaiming her wrist. "You don't want to be here."

"Don't you mean *you* don't want me to be here?" she bit out, yanking free and stumbling back a step. "Why don't you tell me the truth for once, instead of hiding it behind this ridiculous pretense of caring?"

"You want the truth?" he roared. "Fine. I'll give you the truth."

Stepping close, he banded one arm about her waist and dipped to loop the other around her knees. Before she could shriek her protest, he'd bent to swing her up into his arms.

"What are you doing?" she gasped, twisting within his arms and shoving her slim hands against his chest and shoulder. Her floor-length gown, a dizzying blend of champagne and green that matched her eyes, draped over her canted legs while one high heel clattered to the floor. "Put me down!"

"Not a chance," he whispered hoarsely as he strode toward the nearest exit. "I'm taking you out of here before you get eaten alive."

"Stop it," she hissed, her face flushed a ruddy pink. "You're embarrassing me and making a fool of yourself."

"For you? Always," he muttered as he elbowed his way through the doorway.

A shocked murmur of gossip followed them before the ballroom door closed, plunging them into the relative silence of his hotel's lobby.

Within another minute he'd carried her to the relative safety of his private elevator. When the doors slid closed, he gently lowered her to her feet and then punched the button for his office.

He turned back to his wife just in time to see her hand arcing toward his cheek. Her palm cracked against his jaw and fire lit her beautiful eyes. "I hate you," she told him, the crests of her cheeks blazing and her hiked chin quivering. "I wish I'd never met you."

"I don't blame you," he said.

"Then why are you doing this?" she bit out, swiping a knuckle beneath her eye.

"Because—"

"Forget it," she snapped. "I'm angry as hell and I *don't* want to talk about it!"

If his brain had been functioning properly he'd have stepped back and tried to deal with her rationally. He'd have donned a mantle of dignity and control. But for some reason his body wouldn't move away from hers. He was acutely aware of everything about his wife, so close and yet still so damnably far away. Her golden hair, swept up in a glorious, glossy mass. Her breasts, displayed to perfection within the tight bodice of her designer gown. Her mouth, glossed a kissable pink and slightly parted despite her fury.

Damning her for putting him in this position, and himself for not being able to keep her safe, he couldn't force himself to back away. He couldn't force himself to act reasonable and calm.

"You said you wanted the truth," he said, "and that's what I'm going to give you. But not with the whole of England watching."

"You're incapable of telling the truth," she snapped. "And I wish I'd never married you."

The words clawed at his chest, scoring deep wounds he doubted would ever heal. "I'm sure you do." The elevator chimed and the doors slid open, revealing the muted darkness of his vacant office. "Shall we?" he asked, sweeping his arm toward the empty space where she'd rejected him so long ago.

CHAPTER FIFTEEN

COLETTE stalked into his office, her legs trembling with fury. Tears hovered so close to the surface she could taste their salt in the back of her throat. She'd never been so humiliated in her life. After the way that awful, awful old man had looked at her when she'd told him about her marriage to Stephen, she'd wanted to crawl into a hole and simply die. And to have Stephen witness it while she pretended not to notice their obvious rejection of her? It was too much.

"I can't do this anymore," she said, the moment Stephen touched her. "I want a divorce."

He withdrew as if he'd been stung, but then braced his shoulders before stepping toward her again. "All right," he said with a grim nod. "I'll grant you your divorce. After you hear me out."

She sucked in an inhale that felt like shards of glass, her heart clamoring for her to recant the rash words. But she couldn't. It was what she needed to survive. Like ripping off a bandage, it had to be done. Short and swift was better than the agony of seeing his resentment grow by slow, cancerous degrees.

Stephen hadn't turned on the lights, and she was glad of it. She was glad the mellow moonlight slanting through the wide windows cast her in shadow and him in a pale white glow. It illuminated his skin and the startling white edges of cuff and collar, painting him in a wash of silver and glittering blue within his black hair. He was beautiful and she loved him. But tonight had taught her that she could never have him.

"I took you away from my family for a reason," he said, inching close enough for her to catch his scent.

Her body reacted on a visceral level. Wanting. Yearning. She wanted him to touch her, to trail his fingertips over her flushed skin and to taste the seeking warmth of her mouth. She wanted him to make her forget. But she was done dreaming for things she could never have.

"Oh? And what reason's that?"

"It's not what you think," he said. "It's not that you aren't good enough for me." He stepped closer, until his face tipped mere inches over hers. Until his dark mouth hovered so, so close over hers. "Or that you aren't good enough to be a Whitfield."

She gulped a shallow breath while her pulse thudded in the hollow of her throat. Hearing her fears put to words, true though they might be, didn't make them any easier to accept. "I don't care. I never wanted to be a Whitfield anyway."

"I know." He tucked a stray tendril of hair behind her ear, his fingers grazing the skin along the side of her neck. "And I knew it would be even harder to convince you to change your mind after you met my family. I knew they'd make you hate us all."

She stiffened beneath his fingers, though she didn't withdraw. She couldn't make herself abandon the sweet torture of his touch. Not yet. "Only because they hate me."

"They hate me, too. They've hated anything and everything that was important to me since the day I was born."

"Then why—?"

"Do you want to know the real reason I haven't seen Mum's family since her death?"

"What does that have to do with anything?"

"They hate the Whitfields, *all* Whitfields, because of what they did to Mum."

She didn't speak, waiting for him to elaborate.

He inhaled. Exhaled. Then inhaled again, as if trying to rearrange memories he'd buried a lifetime ago. "Mum didn't quite fit the Whitfield mold of what makes a proper wife. She was Irish, she was poor, and she was a barmaid before she married my father."

Stunned, Colette could only blurt, "What?"

"The O'Fallons owned a string of pubs in London's east end, and Mum was their only daughter, born twelve years after their sixth son."

Her thoughts reeled as her previous assumptions about Stephen did a complete one-eighty. "Why didn't you tell me this before?"

"Because I don't like revisiting what happened to her." A grim frown tugged at his mouth. "Mum came from a huge family of loud, brawling men and stubborn, smart-mouthed women. She was a petite black-haired beauty surrounded by a tribe of giant freckled redheads."

Colette simply stared at his face, trying to reframe her perception of Stephen's background.

"Her parents used to claim she was a fairy left behind in exchange for a keg of their best brew."

"But...how did she end up married to your father?"

"Father came in for a pint with some friends, and she served him his beer."

She shook her head, trying to reconcile the Whitfields' past with what all she'd overheard the family say to Stephen. Why would they forbid him to marry someone beneath his station when his own mother had come from such humble beginnings?

"Then why...? I'd have thought he'd choose someone a little more..." She paused, unsure how to proceed. "How does a Whitfield go from being served a beer to marrying the barmaid?"

Stephen's jaw flexed. "Mum was a good Catholic girl and

Father wanted her. Marriage was the only option she'd consider."

"I take it the Whitfields did not approve?"

His expression clouded. "Not at all. Fortunately, Father had reached his majority and he already owned his half of the Whitfield Grand. It was too late to take it back, so the family couldn't do anything to stop him."

"Then that's good, right?"

"No. Since they couldn't do anything to Father, they took their hatred out on Mum. Every chance they had, they told her she was working-class trash, unfit to marry into their lofty ranks of privilege and wealth. They were like sharks, circling for the kill."

Her stomach clenched with empathy. "Your poor mother."

"The Whitfields are a cruel, ruthless lot, no matter the age or gender of their target." He lifted haunted eyes and the odd sheen of vulnerability she saw there made her heart do a queer little twist. "*That's* why I didn't tell them about us marrying. *That's* why I didn't want you to go to the party tonight. It wasn't because I was embarrassed about you. It was because I was protecting you."

He was protecting *her*? "From a few nasty remarks lobbed by people I don't care about? You know I'm tougher than that, Stephen."

Again his gaze shifted back to his hands. Almost as if he were afraid to let Colette see inside. "So was Mum. But she died anyway."

"What?"

"She was at one of Grandfather's birthday parties, a little tipsy and a little more outspoken than usual, when a whole pack of Whitfields attacked her. The things they said to her were awful. Mean and cruel and abusive. They told her she didn't deserve to be one of them and that she'd doomed my father to failure and mediocrity by marrying him. She ran out, crying and unsteady on her feet, and too upset to look where she was going. A car hit her before Father or I could stop her."

Colette simply stared at him in horrified silence.

"Father was never the same after she died. He blamed himself for marrying her, for subjecting her to the monsters that were his family. He stopped eating. Stopped getting out of bed. He forgot he had a son and died six months later." He sucked in a breath and braced his shoulders, appearing strong despite the wounded look in his shuttered eyes. "Fortunately I was big for my age, and good with my fists, and Father had a good lawyer on retainer who was able to protect my inheritance from the Whitfields until I was old enough to protect it myself. But it was not a happy time in my life. I spent much of it scared and alone."

"Oh, Stephen." She understood now. She understood his stubborn refusal to love and be loved. He'd never known the benefits of love; he'd only known the pain. "I'm so sorry." Her heart twisted within her chest and she lifted a hand to his upper arm. As foolish as she was, it was impossible not to touch him.

He shook her off. "Mum had been the world to Father, his reason for living, and he didn't know how to function with her gone. I saw how his need for her made him miserable, how losing her incapacitated him and made him weak. He couldn't even look at me after she was gone because I reminded him of what he'd lost." He swallowed and lifted his gaze to the glass behind her head. "I swore that I'd never let a woman do that to me or any children I happened to have. I swore I'd never be so blind that I chose a wife with my heart instead of my head."

Her heart sank. "So you chose me."

"Yes, I chose you. And I told myself it was with my head. I told *you* the same thing, praying you'd believe it. That you wouldn't run away. You were smart, you were a good mother to our child, and you worked hard. I liked you and you weren't needy. I respected you and I enjoyed your company. You seemed like the perfect choice."

She remained silent, bracing herself for the truth.

"But I lied," he said, his flinty blue gaze returning to roam over her face. Her body. The distance between them became charged, like the expectant silence suspended between the strike of lightning and the clap of thunder. He closed the distance between them, his breath hot against her ear. "I lied to you and to myself. Because my head had nothing to do with my choice."

An awful shaking took up residence in her legs.

"Tonight proved it to me. When I thought I might lose you. When I saw myself repeating the mistakes of my father and not caring." His voice trembled and he braced his arms against the glass behind her, his head dipping low against her cheek. "I married you because I'd be lost without you. I married you because I need you, more than I think I've ever needed anyone. I've been blind with needing you, so much that I couldn't sleep at night."

A crazy blend of doubt and joy filled her heart, winnowing its way through her body and making her hands itch to touch him, to lift his face so she could read the truth in his eyes.

"But I knew you'd never marry me for me. You deserved better than a wretch like me, and I knew it. That's why I didn't hold on to you with both hands when I had the chance. I wanted to spare you the hell of being married to a Whitfield. Of being married to me. But then Emma gave me the perfect excuse to claim you, to take what should never have been mine," he whispered fiercely. "And I'm sorry."

"Stephen—"

"It's not you who isn't good enough," he interrupted. "It's me."

"You're wrong," she said into the trembling silence between them.

He lifted his burning gaze to hers, chips of burning blue ice within a haggard face. A face she loved. "Don't," he ground out. "Don't lie to me."

"Oh, Stephen, you know I'm a terrible liar." Forcing lightness to her tone, she reached to cup his lean cheek. "It's one of my flaws, I'm afraid."

He closed his eyes, turning his mouth to the center of her palm. He rested his lips against it for a moment, his throat bobbing with his swallow before he straightened. "I know I don't deserve to ask this, but I'm going to ask anyway…"

"Yes," she answered, her heart in her throat.

"Yes?" His brow creased with bewildered doubt. "But you don't even know the question."

She reached to cup his dear face between her hands. "It doesn't matter what you ask, Stephen, because I love you. My answer will always be yes."

"You love me?" he asked, his voice a rough, pleading rasp. "Yes."

"But why?" He shut his eyes, and the words worked within his throat. "Why would you love me when I've given you no reason to do so?"

Colette's heart ached for the lonely boy who'd lost both his parents too young, for the lonely man who couldn't associate love with anything other than loss and pain. She dropped her hands to his chest and splayed her fingers wide. "Because inside here, beneath the walls you throw up to keep the world at bay, there's a fine, loyal, good man. Because when you touch me I come alive inside. Because you want to make me happy, even when I frustrate you. Because you're patient and kind and generous. Because you're a wonderful father. You're the other half of me. And because the thought of being without you makes me feel like there's a hole in my chest." She hauled in a breath, feeling the steady thrumming of his heart beneath her palms. "I love you because you're you, Stephen, and because when I'm with you I can be *me*."

"I love you too," he said in a soft rasp. "God help me, I love you too."

The deep confession from his beautiful mouth, those three little words she'd waited a lifetime to hear, set her heart singing with joy. "Tell me again."

"I love you, Colette."

It was so much easier to say than he'd thought it would be. As if the simple exchange of those three tiny, bare words stripped him of all the insecurities and doubts that had plagued him since childhood. And then she smiled at him, renewing his resolve to be the man she wanted. The man she needed him to be.

Stephen gathered Colette up against his chest, hauling her close enough that he could feel her heart beating against his. "I love you," he repeated, the words, now freed, clamoring to be said again and again. Shouted from the rooftops. "I don't know how I didn't see it before."

Nothing he said would be enough to demonstrate his depth of feeling. He'd simply have to show her. Now. And every moment of every tomorrow they ever shared. Dipping his head, he hovered over her sweet lips, sensing her warm smile that curved in response. He backed up just enough to see her hazel eyes, a smile of his own catching at his mouth.

"Don't tease me like that," she breathed, looping her long arms about his neck and trying to pull him back down. "You know I've been wanting for days to kiss you again."

He bent toward her, until nothing but their heated exhalations separated their lips. "Not nearly as much as I," he said. "I've been starved for your kisses, aching for you every hour, every minute, every second that we've been apart."

"Then what are you waiting for?" she gasped breathily.

His laugh rumbled low and deep. "I'm trying to decide whether I want to kiss you shallow, slow or deep." He lifted his hands to her lovely face, cupping her fragile jaw within his palms. "I'm trying to decide whether to start here," he murmured against her trembling mouth, "or here." He slid west, his lips and breath hovering near her dainty earlobe. "Or here," he breathed as he moved his hands to the back of her head, angling her head back and nuzzling the juncture between her neck and shoulder. He rubbed his whiskered chin against the delicate ridge of her collarbone. "Or even here," he teased, and her little gasp sent an arrow of need straight to his groin.

He withdrew enough to peer into her face. Her eyelids had drifted to half mast, her rosy lips parted and her breath coming in shallow pants. He felt her arousal, the eager responsiveness of her body, with every hungry inch of his. And still he tarried.

"I plan to kiss you from head to toe," he promised. "To lick every freckle, taste every crease, and savor every delectable inch of you until you squirm and shout and beg me for more."

She shuddered within his arms, and the fan of her lashes lifted. He felt the heat of her gaze to his knees. "I'm waiting," she whispered.

"I'm here," he said, dipping to gather her up into his arms for the second time that night. "And we're not coming up for air until Emma's got a little sister to torment and tease."

EPILOGUE

"DADDY'S home!" squealed seven-year-old Emma as she launched herself off her stool and raced from the kitchen out onto the tiled marble that led to the front door.

"Daddy, Daddy!" echoed Evie as she raced her older sister toward her father's knees, her sturdy, stocking-clad legs churning fast beneath tiers of red and pink ruffles.

Colette grinned, wiped her hands on her apron, and strode, albeit a bit more slowly than her daughters, to welcome Stephen home. Seeing him at the door, his arms filled with giggling girls and snow dusted over the shoulders of his dark wool coat, she felt a rush of longing and love for the man who'd turned their imposing East Hampton mansion into a home.

Despite all her worries, despite all her fears, she and Stephen had found a way to merge their two visions of what a family and home should be. The warmth and trust between them had transformed the giant colonial house into a happy place full of love and security, where their children could grow, laugh, learn and thrive.

"Daddy, you're cold!" the girls squealed, squirming and shrieking with laughter as Stephen pretended to feast on their necks.

Catching sight of Colette over their daughters' heads, he bent to release the little hellions and they scampered off to the kitchen, calling over their shoulders, "Come and see what we made with Momma!"

"Hey," he said as he slowly straightened, his blue eyes filled with tenderness and love as he leaned to brush a kiss against her cheek. The scent of winter clung to him, a sure sign that autumn had finally relinquished its hold on New York, and the tip of his nose was cold where he nuzzled beneath her ear. "You smell good."

She shivered and arched back with a breathless laugh, pressing her splayed hands against his chest. "And the girls were right. You're cold."

"Care to warm me up?" he asked with a wicked grin, hauling her close enough to bump the hard mound of her belly against his.

"Mmm. That sounds good," she said, threading her arms beneath his coat and around his warm ribs. "Do you think the girls will notice if we disappear for a little while?"

"You know they'd start looking before we got halfway up the stairs."

She snuggled closer. "Parenthood does have its drawbacks, doesn't it?"

The low rumble of his laugh shook his chest beneath her cheek, and she heard the promise of *later*, after the girls were asleep, in his voice. "How was work today?"

"Perfect," she said, leaning back within his arms and beaming up at him. "The girls and I created a lovely new recipe for chocolate pecan squares that Henri is sure to love. And we made enough to send to your mother's family, too."

"Did you, now?" he said with a smile, lifting a hand to brush a stray curl behind her ear.

At the gentle touch, another thread of hope and longing wound itself around her heart, tugging deep within her chest. It amazed her how her reaction to him never seemed to lessen, how her love for him never seemed to dim. "I think they'll like them. I used a splash of Irish Crème in the batter."

"You missed your calling," Stephen murmured, his blue eyes going soft as he stared at her from beneath a fan of black lashes. "With those desserts of yours, you could broker peace for the entire world."

"Oh, I don't know. The girls do far more for peace than my pastries ever could," she said, remembering their first Christmas in London last year.

Their blue-eyed angels had helped ease the transition back into Stephen's maternal family and they hadn't looked back once. The tribe of loud, robust, grudge-holding O'Fallons had been cool and distant—until they'd caught sight of Emma and Evie. One look at their Maggie's adorable grandchildren and the broken bridges and regrets over the past had been set aside forever.

"Those two can melt even the most reluctant of Irish hearts."

"Only because they inherited their mother's beauty."

"I suspect it has far more to do with their father's charm."

"I know better than to argue with a pregnant woman," he teased. The corners of his eyes crinkled as his hands dropped to rest against the burgeoning swell of her belly, idly tracing the ample evidence of her seven-month pregnancy. "How's this little one treating you?"

"He's been kicking up a storm, but I'm holding strong." She placed her hands atop his and waited until he met her eyes again. "He reminds me a bit of his father, you know."

"Me?"

"Mmm hmm," she said with a slow smile. "He has no qualms about letting me know what he wants, when he wants it. I suspect he's going to be a holy terror."

Stephen's mouth hitched in a grin. "Somehow I think you'll be able to handle whatever he throws at you."

"You sound so confident."

"Why wouldn't I be?" he asked, pulling her back into the warm circle of his arms. "You handle *me*."

"I do, don't I?" she teased, tipping her head back and staring up into his smiling blue eyes.

"Oh, yes, you most definitely do," he said, before he bent to catch her mouth in the homecoming kiss she'd been waiting all day to receive.

* * * * *

CLASSIC

Quintessential, modern love stories
that are romance at its finest.

COMING NEXT MONTH from Harlequin Presents® EXTRA
AVAILABLE DECEMBER 6, 2011

**#177 HIS CHRISTMAS
ACQUISITION**
One Christmas Night In...
Cathy Williams

**#178 A CHRISTMAS NIGHT
TO REMEMBER**
One Christmas Night In...
Helen Brooks

**#179 ON THE FIRST NIGHT
OF CHRISTMAS...**
'Tis the Season to be Tempted
Heidi Rice

**#180 THE POWER AND
THE GLORY**
'Tis the Season to be Tempted
Kimberly Lang

COMING NEXT MONTH from Harlequin Presents®
AVAILABLE DECEMBER 27, 2011

**#3035 PASSION AND
THE PRINCE**
Penny Jordan

**#3036 THE GIRL THAT
LOVE FORGOT**
The Notorious Wolfes
Jennie Lucas

**#3037 SURRENDER TO
THE PAST**
Carole Mortimer

**#3038 HIS POOR LITTLE
RICH GIRL**
Melanie Milburne

**#3039 IN BED WITH
A STRANGER**
The Fitzroy Legacy
India Grey

**#3040 SECRETS OF
THE OASIS**
Abby Green

You can find more information on upcoming Harlequin® titles,
free excerpts and more at www.HarlequinInsideRomance.com.

HPCNM1211

Harlequin *Presents*

USA TODAY bestselling author

Penny Jordan

brings you her newest romance

PASSION
AND THE PRINCE

Prince Marco di Lucchesi can't hide his proud
disdain for fiery English rose Lily Wrightington—
or his attraction to her! While touring the palazzos
of northern Italy, the atmosphere heats up...until
shadows from Lily's past come out....

*Can Marco keep his passion under wraps
enough to protect her, or will it unleash itself, too?*

Find out in January 2012!

*Brittany Grayson survived a horrible ordeal at the hands
of a serial killer known as The Professional...
who's after her now?*

*Harlequin® Romantic Suspense presents a new installment
in Carla Cassidy's reader-favorite miniseries,
LAWMEN OF BLACK ROCK.*

*Enjoy a sneak peek of
TOOL BELT DEFENDER.*

*Available January 2012
from Harlequin® Romantic Suspense.*

"**B**rittany?" His voice was deep and pleasant and made
her realize she'd been staring at him openmouthed through
the screen door.

"Yes, I'm Brittany and you must be..." Her mind suddenly went blank.

"Alex. Alex Crawford, Chad's friend. You called him
about a deck?"

As she unlocked the screen, she realized she wasn't
quite ready yet to allow a stranger inside, especially a male
stranger.

"Yes, I did. It's nice to meet you, Alex. Let's walk around
back and I'll show you what I have in mind," she said. She
frowned as she realized there was no car in her driveway.
"Did you walk here?" she asked.

His eyes were a warm blue that stood out against his
tanned face and was complemented by his slightly shaggy
dark hair. "I live three doors up." He pointed up the street to
the Walker home that had been on the market for a while.

"How long have you lived there?"

"I moved in about six weeks ago," he replied as they

walked around the side of the house.

That explained why she didn't know the Walkers had moved out and Mr. Hard Body had moved in. Six weeks ago she'd still been living at her brother Benjamin's house trying to heal from the trauma she'd lived through.

As they reached the backyard she motioned toward the broken brick patio just outside the back door. "What I'd like is a wooden deck big enough to hold a barbecue pit and an umbrella table and, of course, lots of people."

He nodded and pulled a tape measure from his tool belt. "An outdoor entertainment area," he said.

"Exactly," she replied and watched as he began to walk the site. The last thing Brittany had wanted to think about over the past eight months of her life was men. But looking at Alex Crawford definitely gave her a slight flutter of pure feminine pleasure.

Will Brittany be able to heal in the arms of Alex,
her hotter-than-sin handyman...or will a second
psychopath silence her forever? Find out in
TOOL BELT DEFENDER
Available January 2012
from Harlequin® Romantic Suspense
wherever books are sold.

HRSEXP0112

Harlequin® Desire

ALWAYS POWERFUL, PASSIONATE AND PROVOCATIVE.

USA TODAY BESTSELLING AUTHOR

KATHIE DeNOSKY

BRINGS YOU ANOTHER STORY FROM

TEXAS CATTLEMAN'S CLUB: THE SHOWDOWN

Childhood rivals Brad Price and Abigail Langley have found themselves once again in competition, this time for President of the Texas Cattleman's Club. But when Brad's plans are interrupted when his baby niece is suddenly placed under his care, he finds himself asking Abigail for help. As Election Day draws near, will Brad still be going after the Presidency or Abigail's heart? Find out in:

IN BED WITH THE OPPOSITION

Available December wherever books are sold.

SPECIAL EDITION

Life, Love and Family

Karen Templeton
introduces

The FORTUNES *of* TEXAS: Whirlwind Romance

When a tornado destroys Red Rock, Texas, Christina Hastings finds herself trapped in the rubble with telecommunications heir Scott Fortune. He's handsome, smart and everything Christina has learned to guard herself against. As they await rescue, an unlikely attraction forms between the two and Scott soon finds himself wanting to know about this mysterious beauty. But can he catch Christina before she runs away from her true feelings?

FORTUNE'S CINDERELLA

Available December 27th wherever books are sold!